DEADLY CHOCOLATE
ADDICTION

Sally Berneathy

Deadly Chocolate Addiction
Copyright ©2017 Sally Berneathy

Original cover art by Cheryl Welch
http://www.mywelchdesign.com/

Chapter One

My ex walked through the door of Death by Chocolate at ten minutes before three o'clock. Too early for me to close, only a few customers remaining. I couldn't lock him out and I couldn't claim to be too busy to talk to him.

He wanted something. He always wants something and he usually gets it. He's a good salesman. An awful human being but a really good salesman.

On the far side of the room, Paula handed a check to the one couple remaining at the tables. I stood behind the counter watching the last guy there finish his sandwich. I didn't mind watching him. He was hot in a subdued kind of way. Tall, tanned, angular features, but in spite of his casual gray knit shirt and slacks, he could have come straight from a business meeting.

Rick paused inside the door. His blue gaze—a blue as close to the color of the prairie sky as contacts could make it—focused on me.

1

I focused my attention on the man at the counter. "Can I get you some dessert?"

"Absolutely." He looked over my shoulder at the chalk board menu. "What do you recommend?"

Rick took a seat two stools down from my customer.

"Have you been here before?" I asked the man.

His lips tilted upward in an expression almost but not quite a smile and his dark eyes turned hazy. "Years ago, when this place was still Percy's Bar and Grill, I used to come here a lot. It was more bar than grill in those days. Very different menu."

"Percy's Bar and Grill. Yeah, I remember seeing that name as a previous owner when I bought this place. That was a while ago. I've been here for five years, and it was vacant before that." Vacant and kind of a mess. Rick got me a good deal. I suppose I should give him credit for that, but he used up that credit a long time ago. "Was there really a Percy?" I didn't care. I just wanted to keep the conversation going so I could avoid Rick as long as possible.

Percy's former patron nodded. "There was. A short guy with white hair and beard. Friendly enough until somebody got out of hand. Story was, he was a Green Beret in Viet Nam. He never talked about it, but watching the way he dealt with anybody who got out of line, I'd say the story was true."

"I had no idea this place had such a colorful history."

He smiled for real this time. The expression softened the rough angles of his face. "Your place is definitely a change for the better. I like the smell of cookies and brownies better than the smell of cigarettes and stale beer." He looked up at the menu board again. "So, back to dessert. What do you think?"

"For a first timer, I suggest the chocolate chip cookies. We're known for those. We have them with or without nuts, regular or gluten free."

"Sounds great. I'll have one with nuts and gluten."

"Good choice." I served him a large cookie from the display case on the end of the counter.

He took a bite, chewed, and rolled his eyes in ecstasy. "That's really good."

"I could use one of those." Rick's smile beamed from one side of his face to the other. It was so brilliant, it almost flowed into his sun streaked hair...hair that stayed streaked even during the winter months when there was no sun.

I took another cookie from the case, set it on a plate, and shoved it down the counter toward him.

He caught the plate as it slid by. "How are you today, Lindsay?"

You know those anonymous phone calls that begin with *How are you today?* You know immediately it's an annoying sales call. Rick wrote the training manual for those folks.

"I'm fine, thank you. Kind of busy." I gathered up dirty plates and took them to the kitchen. It was only a brief escape. Rick wasn't going away easily.

Paula met me in the kitchen with her load of dishes. "Let me know if you need help." She scraped the food from the plates and set them in the sink then picked up a chef's knife and lifted an eyebrow.

I laughed.

Paula's tiny, seven inches shorter and several pounds lighter than I am. I'm a fierce red-head, she's a peaceful blonde. She's a mother, I own a cat. Well, a cat owns me. Paula's soft-spoken, I shout insults with the best of them. But Paula's the one to be scared of. Just ask her ex-husband who now resides in prison.

"Did the people at the table leave?" I asked.

She nodded. "Everybody's gone except your guy munching on his cookie and, of course, Rick."

"If I can't get rid of Rick in the next five minutes, you're welcome to swoop in with that knife and cut off his…um…hand."

She turned the knife from side to side, studied the blade, and smiled sweetly. Rick would never know what hit him.

I returned to him and my customer.

The guy who once drank alcoholic beverages in my shop before it was my shop looked up from his empty dessert plate. "That was the best chocolate chip cookie I've ever eaten."

"Thank you." I reached for his plate.

He held onto it. "I'll have a piece of your *chocolate du jour*, the Chocolate Caramel Shortbread."

"Sure thing." The guy was tall, dark and handsome to begin with, and he was getting handsomer with every dessert. Yes, Adam Trent is my one and only, but I do like to see a man enjoy my chocolate. I gave him a square of Chocolate Caramel Shortbread.

"Lindsay." Rick had crumbled about half his cookie, but he wasn't eating it. He doesn't really care for chocolate. That alone should have told me marrying him was not a good idea.

I moved slowly, reluctantly, down the counter to stand in front of him. "What do you want?"

"Robin said she'd like for you and your cop boyfriend to meet us for dinner one evening."

"No, she didn't say any such thing. That's totally your idea."

He smiled again. I swear sparks brightened his hair that time. "Maybe. But it's a good idea. She likes you."

"And I like her." First time I'd been able to say that about any of his revolving door list of girlfriends. "She's intelligent, attractive, nice. She'll leave you before long."

Rick didn't bat an eye at the insult. When he's closing in on a sale, he ignores anything that might get in his way.

"We'll go to Pierpont's, my treat."

"No." I got closer than I really wanted to get to him and lowered my voice so my customer couldn't hear the melodrama. "Going to dinner with my ex-husband, his new girlfriend, and my boyfriend is beyond creepy. That's not going to happen. Just tell me what you want, I'll say *no*, you'll leave, and we can save a lot of time."

Rick leaned forward, so close I could smell his expensive cologne. I stepped back. Better the world

5

should hear our discussion than I should get that close to him.

"You and I have history," he said. "We've been together a long time. It's only natural we should want our new friends to know each other. We'll meet for dinner, have a nice steak, a bottle of wine. Of course their desserts won't be as good as yours, but their crème brulee with fresh berries is pretty darn good."

Had he really just said *darn?* He was totally into his clean-cut salesman's act.

"No, we won't. That whole idea is not natural. It's as far from natural as the color of your eyes. Just tell me what you want."

He blinked the eyes under discussion but kept his cool. "You said you like Robin. I might like Trent if I got to know him. I want that opportunity."

"The only way you and Trent will get to know each other is if he arrests you. I can see the two of you spending quality time together at the police station, you in handcuffs, him reading you your rights."

Rick laughed. "You have such a terrific sense of humor. You and Robin are going to get along great." He rose and laid a twenty dollar bill beside his plate. "I'll make reservations for Saturday. Around seven?"

"NO!" I slammed my hand on the counter so hard the dishes bounced.

Damn. Percy should have built a sturdier bar.

Rick's expression became serious. "Lindsay, this is important. I'm trying to help you."

Now we were getting down to it. "What is it this time? You want to buy my house and search for buried treasure? You want me to sign off on some scam that could get us both blown up? Whatever it is, the answer is *no*."

Rick sighed and molded his features into a semblance of sad. "Lindsay—"

"Miss?" The voice of my sole remaining customer. "Those brownies look really good. Do you have one of them with nuts and gluten?"

I moved back down the counter. "Of course."

He gave a knowing wink when I served him the brownie. What a nice guy! He not only loved my chocolate, he was trying to rescue me from Rickhead. It was a gallant though futile effort.

I stomped back to where Rick stood. "Trent and I are not going to dinner with you and Robin. Period. End of discussion. Please leave."

He got that *You're being ridiculous but fortunately I'm a patient man* look on his face. "Now, Lindsay—"

"I believe the lady asked you to leave." Mr. Tall, Dark and Chocolate was no longer eating his brownie. He stood next to Rick. Loomed over him, actually. Rick claims to be six feet tall, but he's actually five eleven and a half. This guy was a good four inches taller and fifty pounds heavier, all of it muscle. I hadn't noticed his biceps when he was eating, but now they bulged from his short sleeved shirt quite menacingly…and attractively.

Rick gave him a disdainful look. "You need to stay out of this, buddy. This is a family matter."

"The judge unfamilied us two months ago." I shoved a finger into his chest. "Leave. Now. Before my friend—" I didn't know my new friend's name, but neither did Rick. "Before my friend, Ransom, gets violent. He just got out of prison and he misses the place. Wouldn't mind going back. A violent assault could get him there."

Ransom lowered his eyebrows and folded his arms. The muscles popped. "Three squares a day and plenty of time to work out. Not a bad place once you establish yourself as top dog, and I'm pretty good at doing that. Ever been in the joint?"

Rick scowled and said nothing. No way would he admit he was intimidated, but his lack of response told me he was.

"Show him your prison tats, Ransom."

"Anything for you, Lindsay." Ransom started unbuckling his belt.

Rick stiffened. "I have to leave now. I have an appointment. But we still have something important to discuss. I'll call you, Lindsay."

"I won't answer, Rick!"

The door closed behind him. I looked at Ransom. He looked at me. We collapsed into laughter.

Paula came over to join us. "Ransom?" she asked. "Where on earth did you come up with that name?"

"Hey," Ransom protested. "I like that name. I'm a Ransom kind of guy. But I'm glad your ex left before I had to show my prison tats. People have been known to faint when they see them." He returned to his stool, took a bite of his brownie and chewed slowly, savoring the flavor.

8

"Thanks for the help with the ex," I said. "He's like a bad penny covered in used bubble gum. Hard to get rid of."

Ransom shrugged. "No problem. It's the chocolate. It gives me super powers."

Paula chuckled. "It must have. Getting Rick to leave is quite a feat. Nice to meet you, Ransom."

I opened my mouth to introduce her, but before I did, he extended a hand over the counter. "Nice to meet you, Paula."

How did he know her name? I didn't recall mentioning it.

Paranoid Paula didn't seem fazed by his knowledge. She shook his hand and headed back to the kitchen.

If she wasn't worried, I shouldn't be.

I took down our largest to-go box. "You need more chocolate in case you encounter a mass murderer or a serial killer on your way home." I opened the display case and began filling it with desserts.

He laughed, the sound deep and rich as my brownies with chocolate chips. "You just met me and already you understand my addiction."

I squeezed one more cookie into the box and set it in front of him. "We get a lot of chocolate addicts in here. I suppose I could start a Chocoholics Anonymous chapter, but why would anybody want to quit?"

Ransom ate the last bite of his brownie and drank the last of his tea. He set the glass on the counter and stared at it. "Yes, I'm a chocoholic. I'm also an alcoholic." He spoke the words calmly, without inflection, but deep emotion resonated in his comment.

I didn't know what to say so I said nothing. Yes, that's a rare occurrence.

He looked up and grinned wryly. "Serving chocoholics is definitely the better choice. I bet you don't have many customers who get into bar fights and break tables or bring out guns and shoot people."

"Yeah, nobody's died in here since I took over." Okay, Rodney Bradford ate chocolate in my place, but he died on the sidewalk out front and he didn't break any tables or shoot anybody so that doesn't count. And Bob died in the back alley before he ate the chocolate I gave him. During my reign, nobody actually died inside the restaurant or as a direct result of my chocolate.

Ransom lifted the lid of his to-go box and peeked inside. "When I used to go to AA meetings, they all drank a lot of coffee. They said an addict is an addict, and caffeine is a better choice of addiction than alcohol. I don't like coffee so I turned to chocolate. No more dancing on the bar or coming home late and passing out on the neighbor's lawn. Now the worst that happens is a smudge of chocolate on my shirt that everybody notices except me." He closed the lid. "I haven't had a drink in over a year."

"You're kidding, right?"

Surely he was.

Maybe he wasn't.

He reached into his slacks pocket and brought out a bronze medallion. "One year."

"Oh. Wow. Congratulations. That's wonderful. Are you serious about the chocolate part? Substituting chocolate for alcohol?"

He slid the medallion back into his pocket. "Yep."

"So you returned to your old haunt, got to eat the best chocolate in the universe, and I got to see my ex running away with his tail tucked between his legs." I paused. "You did know this place had changed ownership and type of beverages served, right?"

His gaze focused on a spot somewhere between my chocolate cream pie and my gluten free brownies. "I knew."

I knew. Two simple words. A statement of fact that was true for every person who came through my door. It was certainly no secret that Death by Chocolate sold chocolate. Why did Ransom's comment sound off-key?

"Do you live around here?" Maybe he'd seen the sign as he drove past on his way to the organic grocery store down the street. He looked like an organic food kind of guy.

"No. I used to live close, but I've been in St. Louis for the last six years."

From his expression, I guessed that St. Louis had not made him happy.

His plate and glass were empty. It was closing time. I should let him take his goodies and go. But he'd run off my ex and he loved chocolate and he looked forlorn. I gave him another glass of tea. Chocolatiers and bartenders also function as amateur therapists.

"What took you to St. Louis?"

"Work. So you've only been divorced a couple of months?"

Apparently he didn't want to talk about St. Louis.

"Legally, yes, but we were separated over two years before Rickhead finally signed the papers." After Fred threatened him with exposure of some of his illegal activities. I looked at the ring on Ransom's left hand. It was scratched, not new and shiny. "Wife stuck with you through the drinking?"

He twisted the ring and gave a brief snort of laughter. Or maybe it was just a brief snort. "She liked me better when I was drinking, when I wasn't paying attention to the things she did." He dropped his left hand to his lap as if he wanted to hide the ring from me…or from himself. "Sounds like you had a bad run too."

I nodded. "Being married to Rick was not the best time of my life."

"But you've found somebody new. A cop? Different sort of guy from the ex?"

Obviously he'd overheard my conversation with Rick. "Yes, he's very different. He's a good guy. Nothing like Rick. Over-the-top honest. Well, I guess you can't be too honest, but he thinks all rules are made to be followed. Like those silly speed limit signs."

Ransom grinned. "Lindsay, don't tell me you drive too fast."

"Never!" I straightened and tried to look innocent. "Never *too* fast. Only as fast as I know I'm capable of going safely. I don't understand why people get so excited about arbitrary numbers painted on a sign."

"But Detective Trent gets excited about those numbers."

Detective? If one has an argument in a public place, one must expect others to listen. I didn't recall referring to Trent as a detective, but maybe Ransom was just using it as a generic term since Rick had referred to him as a cop. "Yes, he gets upset. You'd think I'd broken the law or something."

Ransom was quiet for a moment. I wondered if he was going to get on my case about my driving. "I can tell by the look in your eyes when you talk about him that he's pretty special."

I shrugged and maybe blushed a tiny bit. "He is."

Ransom slid off his stool. "Lindsay, I think you're a really nice person. I hope you and Detective Trent have a lot of happy years together."

"Thank you. And I hope you and your wife can work things out, whatever those things are."

He lifted his left hand and looked at the ring. "We won't, but I appreciate the thought." He reached into his back pocket and withdrew his wallet. "If you'll give me a ticket, I'll pay for this incredible chocolate then leave and let you close."

I lifted both hands in protest. "No! You don't owe me a thing. After what you did for me, I'm in your debt."

He opened his wallet. "It was fun, being an ex-con named Ransom and taking down a jerk. I insist on paying for that privilege as well as the best-in-the-universe chocolate."

I shoved the box of goodies toward him. "I insist you can't pay. Don't forget, I have connections with the local law. You mess with me and I'll call in the cops."

"The cops. Detective Adam Trent." The way he said Trent's name with a combination of nostalgia and respect made me wonder if they'd had a run-in during Ransom's drinking days. He picked up the box. "Thank you very much."

I took the front door key from the cash register and walked around the counter.

He didn't follow immediately and I looked back. He was putting his wallet into his pocket. He smiled guiltily when he saw me watching.

I didn't see any money on the counter, but I'd be willing to bet he'd put it under the plate. Might have known he'd figure out some way to pay.

He picked up his box of chocolate goodies and came to the door then stopped, his gaze fixed on something or someone outside. His lips compressed and his eyes narrowed.

I followed his gaze, expecting to see a terrorist wielding a bomb or a madman with a machine gun or—worse—Rick.

Ordinary people on the sidewalk and ordinary cars in the street.

"I forgot something." He returned to the counter, set down the box, and stood for a moment with his back turned.

Maybe he hadn't left cash before and was doing it now.

He came to the door again. "I'm glad I got to meet you, Lindsay."

"Me too, Ransom. Now that you've found the best chocolate in the universe, I hope you'll return."

A cloud scuttled across the weak October sun and drew a shadow over his face, turning his tanned skin pale. "I hope so too."

He walked away.

I hope so too? That was an odd thing to say.

Or maybe it wasn't.

Maybe Rick's visit had made me paranoid. Maybe I was reading things into Ransom's actions and the way he said Trent's name.

Detective Adam Trent.

Wait a minute.

I looked down the sidewalk. Ransom had vanished.

Making the leap from cop to detective, I could understand. But I had never mentioned Trent's first name. When he and I met, it wasn't under the best of circumstances. I called him by his last name to be disrespectful. It stuck. I never think of him as Adam.

Had Rick called him *Adam*? I wasn't even sure Rick knew Trent's first name.

Ransom knew Trent's first name.

He knew Trent was a detective, not an officer.

He knew Paula's name.

He knew a lot of things for a stranger.

I didn't know anything about him, not even his real name.

15

If he came back, I was going to ask some questions.

I locked the door and returned to the counter.

Under his plate I found a fifty dollar bill. I'd been right about the money. That was sweet. Maybe I was being paranoid after all. I'd been around Rick too long, absorbed some of his suspicious nature.

I picked up the money.

A small brass key lay beneath it.

I lifted the key and studied it.

Perhaps the key had been in his wallet and it got stuck on the bill when he took it out.

He'd looked out the front door and seen something or someone that…what? Startled him? Angered him? Freaked him out?

He'd gone back to the counter.

Had he left the key on purpose?

I couldn't return it. I didn't know where he lived or what his name was. Even Fred couldn't track down someone based on a phony name I'd given the man. At least, I didn't think he could.

What did the key unlock?

If Ransom had wanted me to find something, he'd done a poor job of leaving clues.

I put the key in my jeans pocket and the fifty dollars in the cash register.

Surely he'd return for more chocolate and then we could have a proper introduction and talk about the key.

Surely Ransom would return for the key.

Chapter Two

The evening was uneventful. Rick called five times. I didn't answer five times.

Trent didn't call, but that wasn't unusual. Murder doesn't keep regular hours.

Fred was disappointed I'd given all the leftovers to Ransom, but I made him some fresh chocolate chip cookies—with gluten and nuts—and he was happy.

My cat, King Henry, could have cared less about the lack of chocolate goodies, the mysterious key, or my trauma with Rick. It was fall and mice were scurrying around everywhere, preparing for winter, their activity making them easy prey. He brought me one. I have no idea how many he kept for himself. I didn't ask.

At work the next morning I made a new dessert, Chocolate, Chocolate and More Chocolate Cake.

Lunch rush peaked around twelve thirty. The place was filled with people indulging in chocolate so they could make it through the afternoon business meetings, the censure from their boss, their boring workload, or maybe so they'd have the energy to censure their employees.

I looked up each time the bell over the front door rang, hoping to see Ransom. I wanted to give him back his key as well as see what he thought of my latest *chocolate du jour.*

The bell rang again.

I looked up again.

It wasn't Ransom again.

A woman in tight designer blue jeans and a low cut red silk blouse strode in. She was beautiful, so beautiful several people—especially men—stopped eating and stared at her. She paused and looked around as if appreciating the effect she had on people. People of the male variety. Her blue gaze—a gaze brilliant enough to put Rick's contacts to shame—settled on me.

She strode across the room in my direction, her blond hair swaying smoothly on her shoulders with each step. She was about Paula's size, but the four inch heels on her boots made her appear taller and unnaturally thin, as if a bite of chocolate had never crossed those collagen-enhanced lips. With the heels and her Triple D boobs, I was impressed she didn't tip over.

There were no empty stools. She pushed between two male customers. They didn't complain.

"May I help you?" I asked.

Her collagen curled upward in a phony smile. "You must be Lindsay."

I wasn't admitting to anything, not even my name, without a lawyer or two present. "We're full. Can I get you a to-go order?"

The short, balding man on her left slid off his stool, leaving his chicken salad sandwich half-eaten. "You can have my seat, ma'am."

"Thank you," she purred, "but I'm not staying."

Thank goodness for small favors.

A woman at the far end of the counter waved. I hurried down to her. With her medium brown hair and tailored business suit, she was much easier on the eyes than the artificially enhanced Victoria's Secret model wannabe who insisted I must be Lindsay.

"Would you like some dessert?" I asked the normal woman.

"I would. Can you tell me about the Chocolate, Chocolate and More Chocolate Cake?"

"I'd be happy to. I start with a very moist—"

"Lindsay, we need to talk about your relationship with my husband." Victoria's Secret had a low-pitched voice with sharp edges that cut through all the conversation in the room.

I stopped in mid-sentence and thought of the married men I had relationships with. There was my mother's husband...my father. Unless my sedate father had gone crazy and become a bigamist with very bad taste in women, that wasn't the right husband.

Trent was single.

Although I know nothing of King Henry's past, he's the wrong species for her.

Fred—ah, Fred. For all I know of his past, he could be married. He could be a bigamist or even a trigamist. He is an over-achiever.

"Tunnels of chocolate fudge in the middle, chocolate chips and chocolate whipped cream for the frosting." I finished the description of the dessert, speaking as rapidly as possible. "Would you like a piece?"

"Yes, please."

I had to pass Victoria on the way to the dessert case. "I'll be right with you," I said.

"You'd better because the police are on their way, and they're going to want answers to my question."

She had my attention.

Fred has never admitted to crossing any legal boundaries, but he does hang out with gangsters, hack into government databases, and God only knows what else. In fact, I suspect even God isn't sure about all the things Fred does.

I, on the other hand, occasionally exceed those illogical speed limits posted on ugly signs that deface the landscape. Had I gone over some kind of threshold on the number of tickets a driver is allowed? Was I going to be locked away as a repeat offender? Who'd open cans for King Henry?

I cut a piece of the cake and served the normal lady then came back to Victoria.

She looked at me and smiled.

My mouth had gone quite dry. I desperately needed a Coke. But even more desperately, I needed to know what this woman wanted.

Cops and Fred have a trick when they question people. They remain silent until the person being questioned blurts out something. It always works on me. This time was no exception.

"Is Fred your husband?" I spoke softly, hoping my words would be drowned out by the background conversations.

She folded her arms, lifting the triple Ds so high they threatened to spill out of the front of her blouse.

"Fred? How many husbands are you involved with?" She did not speak softly. I hoped my customers liked my chocolate even if they thought it was prepared by a baker with a giant red letter A for Adultery on her apron.

"Do you need to take a break?" Paula stood beside the counter holding two plates with desserts on them.

I did. I needed to drag Victoria into the kitchen and have this conversation privately. But I wasn't going to. I didn't want to leave Paula alone with the crowd, and I didn't want to be alone with Victoria.

"Thanks, but I'm good."

"Could I get my check?" The man two stools over.

I wasn't sure if I was frustrated or happy about the further delay in my conversation with Victoria. "Would you excuse me?"

I complied with the gentleman's request.

The bell over the front door jingled. I glanced up automatically to see who had come in. The way things were going, it would not have surprised me to see Rick again.

My heart did a happy dance when I saw Trent.

The dance ended with a stumble. He would only interrupt during rush hour for business reasons, cop business.

His grim expression confirmed that this was not a social visit.

Victoria had said the police were on their way.

Had Trent been assigned to haul me off to jail? He had warned me more than once about my driving habits. Well, one particular driving habit.

The woman gave me a smug look then turned and moved swiftly toward the door.

Trying to escape?

She flung herself at Trent.

Ridiculous. He was twice her size. She'd never get past him.

She wasn't trying very hard to get past him.

She wrapped her arms around him and buried her face against his chest.

I flinched. Trent has no problem tracking down the bad guys, hauling them in, beating them with a rubber hose until they confess. Okay, maybe not that last, but he's tough. However, he doesn't know how to handle women in distress. I speak from experience.

I waited for him to push her away.

He slowly detached her but kept an arm around her waist. "What are you doing here?"

"I wanted to see *her*."

He shook his head but let her snuggle against him as they made their way across the room toward me.

Paula stood at a table in the corner, clutching an empty plate, gaze locked on Trent.

Nobody spoke. Nobody even chewed a bite of food. I'd have heard them in the intense silence.

Victoria's words replayed through my brain in an endless loop while my stomach bounced up and down on the floor. *Lindsay, we need to talk about your relationship with my husband.*

Trent?

Had he lied about being divorced?

Not Mr. By-The-Book.

But that would explain his appearance during rush hour and his expression…bleak but determined.

He wouldn't have lied, but he could be wrong about being divorced. That's been known to happen. Somebody thinks the proper documents were filed, but they weren't.

That didn't seem likely either. He was a cop. He had access to all sorts of legal documents.

Had he flown to Las Vegas last night, had too much to drink and…

Not possible.

I prayed it wasn't possible.

"Lindsay," he said, "I hate to bother you, but we need to talk. In private."

Chapter Three

We need to talk. In private.

Nothing good ever begins with those words. They're right up there with: *May I see your driver's license? Do you own a red Celica? Is this cat yours?*

I walked back to the kitchen on feet that weighed fifty pounds each.

"Miss?" a customer called as I passed.

I ignored him. My need to talk to Trent was greater than the customer's need for chocolate.

I entered the kitchen and turned to face Trent. He stepped inside but before the swinging doors closed behind him, that woman followed him in.

Trent looked uncomfortable. I felt uncomfortable. Victoria clutched his arm and smiled. She looked completely comfortable.

"Lindsay, this is Kathleen Gabler. Kathleen is my…" He stopped and cleared his throat.

My own throat closed and my stomach knotted. His what? His *wife*?

This could not be happening. Trusting Trent with my heart had not come easily after my experience with Rickhead. But I had finally given in, admitted to him and to myself that I loved him.

"…my ex-wife," he continued.

Oh, God! He'd said it! She was his wife.

No, that wasn't what he said.

"Your *ex*-wife? You're already divorced?" That was good, wasn't it? Though it still didn't explain the marriage in the first place.

Trent looked confused. "We've been divorced for years. You knew that."

"Oh. Yes. Your ex. Of course." The one he'd dismissed so cavalierly when we first met.

We got married, we lived together for three years, then we got a divorce and stopped living together. Well, actually it was the other way around. We stopped living together and then got a divorce.

What had happened that he suddenly felt the need to introduce me to his ex? I swallowed and prepared to be polite. "Nice to meet you, Vic—I mean, Kathleen." I considered extending my hand to see if she'd turn loose of Trent's arm to shake it.

Nah. Much as I wanted her to release Trent, my aversion to touching her was stronger.

"I just got back in town yesterday." She looked up at him adoringly. "We've been getting reacquainted."

Trent blushed. A hardened cop blushed. Was he embarrassed because she was hanging onto him like a hungry person would hang onto one of my chocolate chip cookies or because I was watching her hanging onto him? "Kathleen's been having some problems." He cleared his throat again. "She came to me for help."

I crinkled my eyes and crunched my lips. I doubt my expression looked anything like a smile, and I didn't care. "That's nice."

"He is nice, isn't he?" She turned her gaze from him to me, from adoring to triumphant. "Adam's letting me stay with him."

Adam had a one-bedroom apartment. I glanced at the carving knife lying on the counter beside me.

Trent wrapped an arm around the woman's shoulders and looked down at her. Seriously? In front of me with a carving knife lying close enough to grasp? "I understand this is a really bad time, Kathleen, but it's going to be all right."

She made a couple of sobbing noises though no tears marred her perfect eyelashes. God didn't make those eyelashes. They were as phony as her boobs.

Trent patted her shoulder. "Why don't you wait in the other room? You don't need to go through this."

I glanced in the direction of the knife.

She shook her head and sniffled. "I have to face it sometime."

He pushed her away gently and reached into his jacket pocket. Was he pulling out his gun? I had only glanced at the knife. I hadn't made any movement to pick it up. Surely he couldn't read my mind.

He withdrew an eight by ten photograph and extended it to me. "Do you know the man in this picture?"

I was glad it wasn't his gun, but it's not a good thing when a homicide cop asks if you recognize someone in a picture.

The photograph showed a smiling couple with palm trees and the ocean in the background.

I recognized both of them.

Ransom and the woman standing in front of me, the one holding my boyfriend's arm.

"Yes, I know him. It's Ransom. He was a customer in here yesterday." I looked at Trent. He wore his cop face, revealing nothing. "Did he do something wrong? He seemed like a nice man. He liked my chocolate."

That woman thrust herself between Trent and me. "He did a lot of things wrong. He beat me and threatened my life. He followed me from St. Louis. He was stalking me."

I was too stunned to react.

Ransom had beaten her? Stalked her? He was a formidable figure, but he'd seemed gentle.

She leaned closer. "Why did you call him Ransom? Did he tell you that was his name?" She shook her head and sighed. "He's such a liar. Why did he come to see you? What did he tell you about me? More lies, I'm sure."

What had he said about his wife? Not much. That she liked him better when he was drunk and didn't know what she was doing.

What had she been doing, other than spending the night with my boyfriend?

Trent laid a hand on her shoulder. Again with the touching. "Kathleen, please wait in the other room. I know you're upset, but this is official police business."

Official police business? I didn't like those words, but I did like that he was ordering her out of the room.

27

She turned to him and smiled. "Of course, Adam. I'm sorry. I didn't mean to cause problems for you."

I'm sorry. I didn't mean to cause problems for you.

Gag.

I'd like to cause problems for her. Shove a stale cookie down her throat and watch her choke. I wouldn't do the Heimlich even if I knew how.

"Just go out front," Trent said. "Paula will get you a Coke or something."

That woman was going to receive the hospitality of my shop? I finally found my voice. "Tell Paula I said to take care of you." Surely Paula would know I meant for her to take care of that woman permanently. Give her an arsenic Coke.

No, we don't really keep arsenic around, but it was a pleasant thought.

Trent ushered her through the swinging doors. Gently. But firmly. Then he turned back to me.

"What's going on?" I demanded.

"I was hoping you could tell me. You may have been the last person to see Jeff Gabler alive."

The last person to see Jeff Gabler alive? When had I lost touch with reality? Since Victoria/Kathleen/That Woman walked through the door, things had become curiouser and curiouser, and, unlike Alice on her trek through Wonderland, I hadn't been eating any mushrooms. "Who? What?"

"The man in the picture, Kathleen's husband. I don't know why he told you his name was Ransom. It's Jeff Gabler. He's dead."

"Dead?" Surely I could come up with sentences of more than one word. "He's dead?" Well, two words were twice as many as one.

"The maid at his hotel found him this morning when she went in to clean."

I leaned back against the counter. Actually, I kind of fell back against it. "Found Ransom?" Two word sentence again. I'd try for three next time.

He nodded. "He was stabbed several times, and his throat was slit."

"And you think I was the last person to see him…" I gulped. "Alive?"

"We don't have exact time of death yet, but it was sometime last night. What time did he leave here?"

For a moment I wasn't sure the counter would hold me. "I don't know." I drew in a deep breath. "Yes, I do. It was after closing time, around 3:30, maybe closer to 4:00. We were talking. I don't remember the exact time."

Trent's cop gaze softened. "Do you want to come down to the station after you close? I'm sorry. I thought this would be a five minute conversation. I had to follow up on the box of desserts in his room, but I figured he was just a customer you wouldn't remember. I didn't realize you talked to him."

"We talked. He ate three desserts. He said…" I hesitated. I didn't want to believe Ransom had abused Kathleen, but his alcoholism might explain that. And he hadn't sworn me to secrecy before he told me. "He said he'd become a chocoholic instead of an alcoholic. He used to drink."

29

"A chocoholic? Good for him. Yeah, he was always a social drinker, but after he and Kathleen married, it got bad."

I could understand why he'd been driven to drink after he married her. But there was something odd about Trent's comments. "You knew him?" Had he been friends with his ex-wife's new husband? Was Rick's suggestion not as bizarre as I thought?

"Jeff and I grew up in the same neighborhood. He was the best man at my wedding. We were friends until Kathleen left me and married him."

"Oh." That went a long way to explaining his grim expression when he came in. "Do his parents still live here?"

"Yes."

"Did you know them?"

"Yes."

Trent's not verbose. But in that single word I heard echoes from his childhood—playing cops and robbers with his friend, running in and out of each other's houses, bonding with both sets of parents.

"Do they know?"

He nodded. "I told them just before I came over here."

"Oh." That completed the reason for his grim expression. "I'm sorry."

"Why don't you come down to the station after you close and give your official statement?" he suggested for the second time.

"Okay."

"I'll see you then." He turned to go.

"Are you taking that woman with you?"

He looked back. "That woman? Kathleen? She came in her own car. She's already been in to give her statement. There's no reason for me to take her with me."

I pushed away from the counter, fully recovered from feeling sorry for him. "Is she going back to your apartment?"

He shifted from one foot to the other. "I don't know. I guess."

"She doesn't need to hide at your place anymore since her dead husband can't hurt her, right?"

"She'll have to get her stuff, but she can do that whenever she wants. I gave her a key."

My mouth opened then closed. I drew in a deep breath. "You gave her a key to your apartment?" Either a pan of cookies was burning or smoke was coming through the top of my head. I hadn't put any cookies in the oven recently. "I gave you a key to my house, but you never gave me a key to your apartment!"

He must have seen the smoke too. He took a step backward. "She asked for one since I leave for work early and she wanted to sleep late. You...you never asked for a key. You've only come to my place two or three times."

"*Two or three*? It was four!" I snatched a dish towel off the counter. "I've got to help Paula. The orders will be backed up by now."

As I strode past him, he reached for me. I slid away and went through the door into the main area.

Paula, standing beside the cash register, gave me a frantic look. I wasn't sure if it was because she had to handle the rush crowd by herself or because she had to serve *that woman* who sat at the counter drinking a cup of coffee and looking evil. She also looked gorgeous, but the evil part predominated. Especially now that I knew she had a key to Trent's apartment.

Paula edged past me to the kitchen.

Trent edged past her into the main area.

Kathleen slid off her stool and strode toward Trent.

Trent looked at me. "Uh, Lindsay, I'll see you at the station around five."

I nodded and watched them leave.

Together.

Something was stuck in my throat even though I hadn't eaten anything in hours.

Was Trent still in love with his ex-wife?

I'd thought I was still in love with Rick for a few weeks after we separated.

Weeks. Not years.

But some men love forever.

Trent was that kind of man.

I just thought it would be me he loved forever.

"Lindsay?" Paula peeked out of the kitchen. "Are you okay?"

"Yeah." I hurried back to help.

Paula handed me three of her tickets and I began making sandwiches.

"What was that all about?" She laid slices of avocado on top of turkey.

"Ransom's dead."

She halted with a slice of bread a few inches from the top of the sandwich. "What happened?"

I gave her a quick summary.

Paula's good at remaining calm. She didn't faint or gasp or freak out, not even when I told her about that woman having a key to Trent's apartment.

She hefted a tray loaded with four plates. "Did you tell Trent about Rick's visit?"

"No, I didn't even think about it. With everything going on, Rick never crossed my mind."

"You probably should tell Trent. Rick and Ransom had an unfriendly encounter and then Ransom was murdered."

I cringed. I didn't want to tell Trent about Rick's insane suggestion that had led to our argument and the *unfriendly encounter* between Rick and Ransom. "Rick's visit had nothing to do with Ransom's murder. There's no point in bringing it up."

She looked at me for a long moment. "At least Trent didn't keep his ex's visit a secret."

My jaw dropped. "I can't believe you just said that! It's not the same thing! Rick did not spend the night with me, and Trent didn't tell me about Kathleen voluntarily. She charged in here like a Victoria's Secret model on meth. He had to tell me!"

Paula ignored me and pushed through the door.

I picked up my tray of food and followed.

As usual she was right. I had to tell Trent about Rick's visit and why Ransom had run him off.

Damn.

Chapter Four

I went to the police station after work to tell my boyfriend about his ex's second husband's run-in with my ex. It sounded like an episode from a television talk show. Could my life get any more melodramatic?

The official interview was conducted in a totally official manner in an official interview room with Trent's partner, Detective Gerald Lawson. When it was over, I left before Trent could become unofficial. I'd had my quota of confessions for the day.

I got home late. King Henry was waiting. He gave me an icy blue stare then turned and stalked haughtily toward the kitchen. He knew I was late. He can tell time, though I think he only looks at the digital readout on the DVD player. I don't think he can tell the time on a regular clock.

But I'm not certain.

I followed him. "I have a good excuse."

He sat beside his empty bowl. He wanted food, not excuses. I gave him both. He ate the former and ignored the latter then asked to go outside and play with the neighborhood mice.

I let him out, grabbed some cookies, and went to Fred's. No need to call him. He's either psychic or has every house in the neighborhood bugged. He'd be waiting for me.

He was.

He opened the door before I could ring the bell. "I'm sorry about your friend," he said.

I entered and handed him the bag of cookies. "Are you talking about Trent or Ransom?"

His eyes widened slightly behind his wire-rimmed glasses. "Trent?"

"Aha! You don't know everything." It was a small victory in a day of losses.

He closed the door behind me. "Of course I don't. What's going on with Trent?"

I crossed Fred's immaculate hardwood floors to his immaculate leather sofa, sat and picked up the crystal glass of red wine waiting on a coaster on the immaculate oak coffee table.

He retrieved his half-empty glass and sat in his recliner.

I sipped the wine. Excellent, of course. "How did you know I'd be coming over and would need wine?"

He arched a white eyebrow toward his immaculate white hair. "Last night you told me a story about a new friend and today that new friend is dead. I wasn't sure what time you'd get here, so I opened red wine instead of a chilled white."

He always tries to make his psychic abilities sound normal.

"Trent's ex-wife is sleeping with him and he gave her a key to his apartment and they got a divorce because she left him for his best friend who was murdered today and maybe he's still in love with her." I chugged the wine and set my empty glass on the coaster.

Fred stood, poured me another glass, and sat down without a word.

"You didn't know that, did you?" A triumphant but painful gloat.

"Of course I didn't know that until you told me. Where did you come by this information?"

"He told me."

The arched eyebrow rode higher. "He told you he may still be in love with his ex?"

I drank more wine. "Not exactly."

"When you say Kathleen Gabler is sleeping with him—"

"How do you know her name?"

"I checked Trent thoroughly when you first showed an interest in him. Surely you didn't think I'd let you become involved with someone I didn't approve of."

Should I be flattered that he cared or insulted because he didn't trust my judgment in men?

That was an easy one. Who'd trust my judgment after Rick? Certainly not I!

I sat forward, cradling the bowl of my wine glass in both hands. "What did you find out about her? Did her husband really abuse her or did she abuse him? Was she ever in a mental hospital?"

"I don't know. I didn't check on her. You weren't involved with her, and I didn't find any communication between Trent and her after the divorce. She married Jeffrey Gabler immediately, he got an offer to set up a branch law firm in St. Louis, and they moved."

I sat back. I'd hoped he'd have some dirt on that woman. "Trent said he and Ransom grew up together. Ransom was his best man when he married Kathleen. And I thought my divorce was the stuff of soap operas."

"Most divorces are."

"Are you speaking from experience?" Had he been through a soap opera divorce? Was I finally going to learn something about Fred's past?

"I'm speaking from watching the Investigation Discovery channel on TV. The term *friendly divorce* is an oxymoron."

"There's nothing friendly about that woman. I think she killed Ransom. Easier than another divorce. She spent the night with Trent. She's using him for an alibi, and he's letting her."

"If she was with Trent when the murder occurred, how could she have done it?"

Sometimes I hate it when Fred's logical. "I don't know how, but I intend to figure it out."

"It's unlikely she killed her husband. The room was torn apart, his wallet and watch stolen. It appears it could have been a simple robbery. Somebody he met in the hotel bar, maybe."

"He wouldn't have gone to the bar. I told you he quit drinking a year ago."

Fred shrugged. He didn't seem very interested in helping me prove Kathleen was guilty of murder. "He was from this area, grew up here. I'm sure he still has friends and family. He could have arranged to meet somebody in the bar even if he wasn't going to drink."

"Why would his friends or family kill him? No motive. Kathleen had a motive."

"What motive?"

"So she wouldn't have to get a divorce. Maybe they had a pre-nup and she wouldn't get anything. If we can prove she did it, Trent won't let her stay with him."

"Yes, I suspect that is a true statement. That brings us back to my original question. When you say Kathleen Gabler is sleeping with Trent, are you using the word *sleeping* in a literal sense or as a euphemism for sexual interaction?"

I blinked. Twice. Took another drink of wine. Fred and I had never discussed the "s" word. "I don't know. There's only one bed in his apartment."

"He also has a sofa."

"How do you know that?"

"Most people do. Does he not?"

"Yes, he has a sofa." I knew where this was going. He was taking Trent's side.

"As I recall, Trent slept on your sofa until your divorce from Rick was finalized."

I gazed at my almost empty wine glass and nodded.

"Trent has an extremely well-developed sense of honor, of right and wrong."

I nodded again.

"He won't even fix your speeding tickets because it would be wrong."

I glared at Fred. "It would not be wrong. Are you defending him or trying to make me even madder at him?"

"I find it unlikely that a man so fixated on doing the right thing would sleep, in either definition of the term, with his ex-wife while he's in a committed relationship with you."

He was making sense. I wanted to believe him. But I wasn't through being mad at Trent for letting that woman inside his apartment. "Why would he give her a key? He's never given me a key."

"Did you ask for one?"

"No."

"She probably asked."

"She did, and he gave it to her."

"If you ask him for one, he'll give it to you."

"That is not the point!"

"Did you tell Trent about the key Ransom left for you?"

In all the drama of the day, I had forgotten. The only key on my mind had been the one Trent gave Kathleen. "I didn't even think about it."

"Where is it?"

"Still in the pocket of yesterday's jeans."

"Since Ransom was murdered hours after leaving that key with you, it could be important. You should give it to Trent."

"Whatever." I'd deal with that later. "Let's get back to the key we know about, the one Trent gave Kathleen. Can you find out if they're…you know."

"No, I don't know."

Of course he knew. Fred was being deliberately obtuse. That did not improve my mood. "Sleeping in the same bed. Having sex."

"Don't be ridiculous. The only way I could find out about that would be if I put a camera in his bedroom."

I finished my wine and set the glass precisely in the center of the coaster. "Okay."

He rolled his eyes. "I have lasagna in the oven and homemade bread for garlic toast. Are you interested?"

"Of course."

He didn't say he would put a camera in Trent's bedroom, but he didn't say he wouldn't.

Chapter Five

It was dark and moonless by the time I left Fred's. With the combination of his common sense advice, lasagna, and wine, I felt better about everything. Well, everything except Ransom's death.

I climbed the four steps to my front porch. Light was out again. I turned to wave at Fred who always watched until I got inside where he could watch over me through the hidden camera he claims doesn't exist.

A shadow moved on the other side of the porch. I froze then sneered at myself. Porch swing on that side. Wind moving it.

Except there wasn't any wind.

"Lindsay, it's me. Don't be scared."

In the depths of the shadows I saw a darker shadow with bright blue eyes and streaked blond hair that shone even with no moonlight. "Damn it, Rick!" I'd rather have seen a burglar or a serial killer. "What are you doing here? Did you turn off my porch light so I wouldn't see you?"

"I just unscrewed it."

"So I wouldn't see you. Where's your car?"

"I parked up the street."

I spread my hands in frustration. "So you turned off my light and hid your car because you knew I wouldn't want to see you, then you waited on my front porch to ambush me? If I'd wanted to talk to you, I'd have answered one of your dozen calls."

"Lindsay—"

"Go away!" I unlocked my door and pushed it open.

"This is about chocolate!"

I hesitated. I couldn't help it. Automatic reaction to that word.

Rick saw my hesitation and swooped in for the salesman's close. "You always use quality chocolate. I've found a source where you can get same quality chocolate for half what you're paying now. As much chocolate as you use, that's going to be a significant savings."

Don't listen to him! a voice inside my head shouted. *Go inside and lock the door! Blockade it with a bookcase! Put your hands over your ears!*

I froze in place, seduced by visions of all that lovely chocolate.

Rick moved closer and whispered a few brand names. "It's the real thing, just seconds. A bar of sixty percent cacao with one corner broken. Chocolate chips that aren't uniform size. You don't care about that sort of thing since you're going to melt the bars and put the chips in cookies and cakes."

"What about cocoa?" I was done for! I'd shown an interest. I'd talked to him. My signature was almost on the dotted line.

"Absolutely. Tons of it. Dark and pure. Let's go inside and talk."

The visions of chocolate crashed to the ground. "No. You are not getting inside my house. It's too hard to get you out! Five minutes inside and it's like you've established squatter's rights!"

I turned to face him.

From the corner of my eye I saw a ghostly form sliding along the ground through the darkness, approaching the porch at a rapid rate. King Henry. Just in time to rescue me.

He dropped a mouse at my feet then snarled at Rick. My cat has much better insight into people than I do. He never liked Rick.

"That's disgusting." Rick took a step backward, away from the mouse and—though he'd never admit it—away from Henry's half inch fangs. Rick fancies himself a lover, not a fighter. Speaking from experience, he's not very good at either.

"It's late," I said. "I have to get up early."

"I'll call you tomorrow and we can continue this discussion."

"Or I can call you."

"You seem to have memory loss when you say you'll call me. I'll call you."

He would. And call me. And call me. He didn't get to be top agent at Rheims Commercial Real Estate by giving up.

If I called him, at least I could control the time.

"I promise I'll call you tomorrow as soon as I get a minute. But if you start calling me over and over, I'm not going to answer, and I'm not going to call you."

"If you haven't called by closing time, I'm coming over."

I thought about pointing out that threatening me was not a good way to get me to agree to his scam, but I'd wasted enough time talking to him.

"Okay." I slipped into my house, grateful to have escaped, albeit by a narrow margin.

Henry gave one final snarl and followed me in.

I closed the door and leaned against it, listening to Rick's footsteps as he left the porch.

Henry wound around my leg.

I scanned the immediate area to be sure he'd left his evening's catch on the porch. With any luck, some other critter would steal it during the night.

"Thank you," I said. "You deserve some catnip. But you did wait until the last minute, until he had time to weave a spell. You could have run him off before I got home."

Henry heard only the catnip part. He trotted toward the kitchen, tail waving happily as he contemplated his drug of choice.

As soon as my cat was properly stoned, we went upstairs to bed. I took off my blue jeans and chocolate-stained shirt. I wore an apron while baking but somehow I always got chocolate on my clothes.

The stains reminded me of something Ransom had said. *Now the worst that happens is a smudge of chocolate on my shirt that everybody but me notices.*

He'd been wrong. The worst that happened was his murder.

And Fred thought the key he left could be important.

I lifted yesterday's jeans from the hamper and extracted the small key then sat on my bed and studied it.

Had Ransom known he was going to die and left a clue to his murder?

He had seemed upset after he looked out the door. Had he seen his murderer?

Had Kathleen been spying on him?

Maybe he left it with me so Kathleen couldn't get her hands on it. Maybe he didn't want her to find…what?

It would have been nice if he'd left a note with the key, a note telling me what to do with it.

His visit to Death by Chocolate had not been a coincidence. He knew who I was.

Fred was probably right. I should give it to Trent. Ransom had questioned me about my relationship with his former friend. We'd discussed Trent's honesty. He would have been sure Trent would do the right thing with this key.

Whatever that might be.

I sighed and leaned back on my pillow.

More likely it was an unimportant key that had slipped from his wallet.

I wanted it to be significant, wanted it to be a clue that would incriminate that woman.

I wanted an excuse to call Trent and find out if she was still at his apartment. The key was the perfect excuse.

From the foot of my bed Henry gave a soft snore. I took that as approval.

But I needed to do one thing first.

I called Fred.

"Are you in bed yet?" I asked.

A moment of silence.

Had I interrupted something? Was Sophie from across the street with him? I've never been able to catch them doing anything interesting together, but that doesn't mean they're not. It just means I haven't caught them yet.

"No, I'm not in bed. Do you have a reason for asking?"

"Yes. I need you to make a copy of Ransom's key before I give it to Trent."

"You do realize you called your neighbor, not the local hardware store."

"I would not call the local hardware store and ask if they were in bed. I'll bring you the key in about ten minutes, as soon as I call Trent and tell him about it. You can keep it overnight and make a copy."

"All right." He hung up. Fred's a busy man. He doesn't have time to say good-bye.

One of these days, I'm going to figure out what he's so busy doing.

Now to call Trent. I usually call his cell number, but he'd be the only one to answer his cell. If I called his land line and Kathleen was there, she might answer. He only has one phone for that land line and it's on the nightstand beside his bed.

Trent answered on the second ring.

"Hey," I said. "You busy?"

"Hi, lady." His voice had a slight lilt, as if he was glad to hear from me. That was a good start. "Just watching a little TV. What's up?"

"Ransom left a key yesterday."

"A key? A key to what?"

"I don't know. I found it under his plate after he left. I think maybe he wanted to get it to you. This may sound paranoid, but I don't think he came into my place by chance."

I waited for him to say I sounded paranoid, that Ransom had come to my place because he used to drink at Percy's, because he liked chocolate, because he was in the neighborhood.

"Go on."

"He knew Paula's name before I introduced them, he called you a detective instead of an officer, and he knew your first name."

"You didn't mention any of that when you gave your statement today."

"I didn't think about it. I had other things on my mind."

"And the key."

"I forgot about it." The only key I was thinking about during that time was the one he gave Kathleen, and I wasn't going to tell him that. "Do you think the key may be important?"

"I'll drop by your place tomorrow and pick it up."

Tomorrow was the logical time. It was late, I had to get up early, and I needed to get the key to Fred tonight. But I wanted Trent to assure me Kathleen wasn't there without asking him directly. "Or you could come by here tonight and pick it up."

"I could. Do you want me to come by tonight? It's already past your bedtime."

47

Even if she was there, he was willing to leave her. "No," I said. "It's late. Tomorrow's fine."

"Then I'll see you tomorrow." He paused. "Now that Kathleen doesn't have to worry about the possibility of Jeff coming after her, she went to a hotel."

I didn't realize how tightly my gut was clenched until it unclenched.

Henry gave a short burst of purring. Having a happy dream or had he heard Trent? Cats have exceptional hearing, plus they're psychic.

"You and Ransom…Jeff…were friends. Do you believe he hit her?"

"I don't know. Two days ago, I'd have said no. The Jeff I knew was a soft-spoken, gentle guy, but people change."

"Obviously. I'll bet when you two were picking out tuxedos for your wedding, you never expected him to steal your wife."

For a long moment he said nothing. Was my comment too personal? Was I being too nosy? I've been accused of that, but Trent and I have a personal relationship so I felt entitled to ask personal questions.

"You've met Kathleen," he finally said. "He didn't have to steal her. She went voluntarily."

"So you're not angry with Ransom? You didn't lie awake at night and plot his downfall?"

"Do you plot the downfall of the woman Rick left you for?"

"Ending up with him was enough punishment for her. But she was a stranger. Ransom was your friend."

"Yeah, that hurt. We grew up together, the four of us…Jeff, Kathleen, Gary, and me."

"Gary?"

"Gary Durant. He's a lawyer with the same firm Jeff worked for. He's still with the Kansas City branch."

"He and Ransom were both lawyers?"

"We were all going to be attorneys, move up in the world."

"All of you? Kathleen too?" Somehow I couldn't see her slogging through law books, doing research for a brief, appearing in a courtroom in front of a judge in her four inch heels, tight jeans, and low cut blouse.

"Not Kathleen. She didn't have the grades or the desire to get into law school, but she did have the desire for a better life. None of us had a lot, but Kathleen had it the hardest. Her dad left when she was ten. There were five kids in her family, and her mom had a tough time making ends meet."

If he was trying to make me feel sorry for her, it wasn't working. "So she decided marrying an attorney would be the next best thing."

"We got married my first year of college." His response validated my theory. "I have to give her credit," he continued. "She worked as a waitress while I was in school."

"But then you decided to be a cop instead of a lawyer," I guessed, "and Kathleen left you for someone with more earning potential?"

"It sounds pretty cold when you say it like that."

"Yeah, it does. How would you say it?"

He was silent for so long I thought we might have been disconnected.

"Never mind," I said. "You don't have to tell me. I'm not trying to be nosy." *Not like I'm your girlfriend and entitled to know things like that.* I was torn between wanting to feed him stale brownies or cry.

Maybe both.

"I wasn't a great husband."

I waited a few seconds and finally realized I'd be waiting a long time if I expected him to expound on that statement. "Can you be a little more specific? Did you eat crackers in bed? Criticize her cooking? Sleep in the other bedroom?"

"I was going to school and working as many hours a week as I could delivering pizza. That didn't leave a lot of time for Kathleen."

"Are you seriously making excuses for that woman?"

"I guess I feel a little guilty about what happened."

Henry snorted in his sleep. Definitely psychic.

"I do not believe you just said that. Your wife left you for another man, and you feel guilty?"

"It worked out all right for her. Jeff made partner fast and was sent to St. Louis to start a branch firm. She got to be a rich lawyer's wife for a few years."

How special for her. "What went wrong?"

"I don't know. I hadn't heard from either of them for years until he called yesterday afternoon and left a message. Said he was in town and wanted to get together."

"You didn't mention that you'd talked to him."

"I didn't call him back."

I clenched my phone so tightly I expected it to break or at least bend. He didn't want to talk to his friend. He hadn't forgiven him for stealing Kathleen. Did that mean he regretted her loss?

"You didn't return his call?"

"I thought about it. I thought too long. She showed up at my front door claiming she was terrified that Jeff had followed her here, checked into the same hotel she did, and was going to kill her."

"And you believed her?" I didn't. I'd only met Ransom once, but I didn't believe he planned to kill his wife.

"He followed her to Kansas City. He came to town and checked into the Pleasant Grove Manor. His parents didn't even know he was here. This wasn't a regular visit."

I couldn't argue with that. "Why did she come to you? I wouldn't go to Rick if I was being pursued by a zombie and Rick had the only house with a door on the entire planet."

He chuckled. "You'd stand your ground and kick that zombie's butt. Kathleen's not as strong as you, and she doesn't have the friends you do. I'm the only person she felt she could turn to."

Because I have friends and I'm not weak and wimpy, Kathleen was entitled to special treatment? I bit my tongue to keep from saying that. "Okay, I just have one more question."

"Yes, she gave me back the key to my apartment."

"I wasn't going to ask that." Though I'd wanted to. "My question is, who bought the boobs, you or Ransom?"

He laughed. "Jeff did."

"I'll see you tomorrow. I'm making Raspberry Chocolate Bundt Cake. I'll save you a piece."

We hung up and I headed to Fred's house. The night was chilly and I probably should have grabbed a jacket, but I only had to go a few feet.

He was waiting at the door when I got there. I handed him Ransom's mysterious key.

"Come on in for a minute."

I shivered and wrapped my arms around myself. "Thanks, but I'm going to run home and go straight to bed. It's been a long day."

"You need to come in. I made you a cup of hot chocolate."

Fred's hot chocolate may not be as good as mine, but it's close.

I went inside.

Two steaming mugs waited on the coffee table. I sat down and lifted mine in both hands, savoring the warmth and aroma before tasting.

"Kathleen Marie Gabler began life as Kathy Ann Johnson."

"Her name's as phony as her boobs and eyelashes."

"She had it legally changed when she was eighteen."

"How old was she when she had her boobs changed?"

Made him blink, but only once.

"Twenty-four. She was the youngest and only girl of five children. Dad left when she was ten."

Trent had already told me that, but I didn't want to appear ungrateful for Fred's efforts. I nodded and sipped my cocoa. Extraordinary. Somehow he'd found my recipe. Probably hacked into my brain.

"The mother had no marketable skills. Actually, I should say she had no legal marketable skills. She was arrested a couple of times for prostitution, but they let her go. Two older brothers dropped out of school and left home."

Damn! I was starting to feel sorry for Kathleen. I didn't want to feel sorry for her. I wanted to feel justified in hating her.

"After she married Jeff Gabler, her fortunes improved dramatically. While he was working and schmoozing with the clients and other partners, Kathleen partied, traveled the world, bought expensive clothes and jewelry. About a year ago Jeff sobered up and realized they were broke and in debt. He took away her credit cards and started working to get things straightened out, but she still racked up the bills. Two weeks ago he filed for divorce."

I drank more hot chocolate and considered this new information. "So she married him for money, and now the money's gone and he filed for divorce. If that happened, she'd get nothing because they're broke right now but he could continue to work and earn money. I think we've found her motive. Did he have life insurance?"

Fred nodded. "One policy from work for a million and another personal for a second million."

"There you go. She killed him for the insurance."

"Only a few hours ago you were upset because she was sleeping with Trent when her husband was being murdered. Have you come up with a way she could have been in two places at one time?"

"Easy. She hired a hit man. With two million dollars at stake, I'm sure she could find somebody. I can't wait to tell Trent. He's going to freak out that he let a murderer spend the night with him."

"Maybe you should have a little more evidence before you say anything to Trent."

"He's the cop. It's up to him to find the evidence."

"I'm glad you have that attitude. I was afraid you'd feel compelled to prove to Trent that his ex-wife is a murderer."

I shrugged. "The facts speak for themselves. Ransom was going to divorce her and leave her with nothing. He had two million in life insurance. He was worth more to her dead than alive." I tapped my cup with my fingernail and frowned. "She said he abused her. I don't believe that. Did she ever call the cops on him?"

"There's no record of any domestic violence."

"I knew she was lying. Ransom had kind eyes. You should have seen *her* eyes. That woman's cold. She'd be more upset about breaking a fingernail than about killing somebody." I lifted a hand to stop any further argument from him. "I know what you're going to say. Why did he follow her to Kansas City if he wanted to be rid of her? I haven't figured that one out yet, but I know he had a good reason."

"Actually, the question is, who followed who? Jeff arrived two days ago. You indicated Kathleen came to Trent's house yesterday evening."

"Oh."

"He didn't tell you why he was visiting Kansas City?"

"No. He didn't say, and I didn't ask. I didn't want to be nosy."

Fred laughed. Actually, he pretty much guffawed. I've never seen him laugh so hard.

I lifted my chin indignantly. "Hey! I bet I know something you don't."

He wiped his eyes and resumed his usual haughty demeanor. "Go on."

"He didn't tell his parents he was in town."

"You're correct. I did not know that. You must have done a good job of being nosy."

"I did not. Trent told me that voluntarily."

"So he came to town and didn't tell his parents, but he did call his wife's ex-husband."

I waited. He said nothing more. "What does that tell us?" I finally asked.

"I have no idea."

"He came to town to hide from Kathleen," I speculated. "He called Trent because he knew Kathleen was planning to kill him and he wanted to find out how Trent survived being married to her."

"Kathleen didn't kill him. She has an alibi...your boyfriend."

I sat straighter, more resolute. "You seem to be forgetting about the hit man. All we have to do is figure out who she hired."

"What happened to letting the cops find the evidence?"

I finished my hot chocolate, set the cup back on the coaster, and glared at Fred. "I changed my mind."

"You do realize you may prove your arch enemy's innocence."

"No. We're going to prove her guilt. She won't be able to sleep with Trent when she's in prison."

Chapter Six

The next morning as Paula and I prepared for the breakfast crowd, I told her about my conversations with Trent and Fred.

Paula smacked her yeast dough especially hard. "I could have told you that woman has never been abused."

Paula knows whereof she speaks. Her three-year old son Zach is the only good thing that came out of her relationship with Zach's father. When I first met Paula, she had just run away from that relationship and was terrified of the world and everybody in it. Kathleen showed none of that fear.

I poured raspberry liqueur into my batter then took a drink just to be sure it was okay. "The way I've got it figured, now that she's going to get all this money from Ransom's life insurance, she can be rich and have her first love, Trent."

Paula spread the dough and picked up her rolling pin. "Even if she isn't arrested for murder, she'll soon be going back to St. Louis to take care of all the estate stuff. Besides, Trent's not going to get mixed up with that skank again."

Skank was not a word I'd ever heard Paula use before. I used it often in referring to Rick's women. She probably learned it from me. I gave myself a mental pat on the back for increasing her vocabulary.

"Thank you," I said. "Calling my boyfriend's ex-wife a skank is a sign of true friendship."

❧

The breakfast crowd had cleared out and the lunch crowd had not yet started to arrive. Paula and I were in the kitchen slicing roast and baking cookies when the front door bell jingled.

"I'll get it." I shoved a pan of cookies into the oven, set the timer, and pulled off my apron. "It may be Trent coming by to get Ransom's key." I pushed through the kitchen door and into the main room of the restaurant.

Kathleen did her runway model thing across the floor to the counter. "I was hoping to get to talk to you alone."

I moved behind the counter. "Funny how that works. I was hoping I wouldn't get to talk to you alone or with somebody."

She eased onto a stool and set her designer handbag on the counter then fixed her cold marble gaze on me. "Your friend came to see me last night."

First I was hanging out with her husband, now my friend was hanging out with her. "Are you talking about Henry?"

Her smile tilted into an arrogant smirk. "He didn't leave a name."

"If you spent the night under a bridge in my neighborhood, it was probably Henry. About eighteen inches tall, white hair with gold markings, big blue eyes? I hope you didn't let him get too close. He has rabies."

Her entire face twisted into an ugly scowl. She leaned forward and tapped the counter with one long, red fingernail. "You need to back off. You're way out of your league. Let me explain it to you. This can go one of two ways. You can stay out of my way and when the investigation into my husband's murder is over, I'll give Adam back to you and leave town." She pointed the fingernail at me. "If you keep messing with me, I'll take him back. You need to tell your creepy friend to stay away from me. I told him I don't have the key anymore, that I gave it to you. But of course I lied. I've still got it." She patted her designer bag and smiled smugly.

"The key?" I slid a hand into my pocket. The object in question was still there. "You don't have the key."

"Did Adam tell you I gave it back to him?" She laughed. Cackled, actually. "I'm sure that's not the first time he's lied to you, and it won't be the last. I've known Adam a lot longer than you have. You'll never know him the way I do. Yes, I still have his key, and I was back in his bed last night after your friend's visit to my hotel room. It gave me the perfect excuse, thank you very much."

Icy fingers gripped my chest, two of them. Fingers, not chests. One cold digit for her comment that she'd gone back to Trent's bed, the second because I suddenly realized we were not talking about the same key. I was talking about the key in my pocket. She was talking about the key to Trent's apartment.

He told me she gave back his key. And I believed him. Still believed him. Kathleen was lying.

I was certain of it.

I was.

Certain.

No doubt in my mind.

But what was the business about a friend of mine coming to her room and asking her about the key? Fred had the ability to break into her room, but he had no reason to do it.

She made up the entire thing so Trent would think she needed protection.

So she would be able to get back in his apartment.

Well, she wasn't the only one who could make up stories.

"I'm surprised you saw my friend. He can usually sneak in and out without waking anybody. He got what he came for, a sample of your DNA. What do you think *Adam's* going to say when he finds out your DNA matches the skin cells on that earring the police found in your murdered husband's hotel room?"

She lifted her hands to the diamonds dangling from her ears and went pale at that accusation. Well, she started to go pale. Maybe.

Okay, before I could assess her reaction, the bell over the door jingled and Trent walked in, stopped, and looked from one of us to the other. I studied him closely for any sign of guilt. Nothing. He had on his cop face. Didn't mean he wasn't guilty. Just meant nothing showed.

"Lindsay, Kathleen." Cop voice. No emotion. "What are you doing here?"

"I own this place!" I protested.

He frowned. "Not you."

Kathleen slid off her stool and started toward him. "I called the station and they said you were coming over here." Her voice had become kittenish and cloying. "I needed to see a friendly face. Last night was so awful."

If last night was awful, at least I knew they didn't have sex last night.

She flung herself at him, wrapped her arms around him, and made sobbing noises.

Trent patted her on the back then pushed her away and held her at arm's length. "I know this is hard for you, losing your husband in such a terrible way and then an intruder in your room. You should get some rest."

Kathleen gave a huge sniff. "Yes, I need to rest. But I can't go back to that hotel room after what happened there." She gave him the full force of her pitiful gaze. "Your apartment feels so safe. I know I could rest there."

"Trent," I said before he could cave, "I need to talk to you." I tilted my head toward the kitchen.

He nodded and started my way...with that woman attached to his arm. "Kathleen, I need to talk to Lindsay in private. Can you give us a couple of minutes?"

She released his arm. "Please hurry back. I think somebody followed me here." She bit her lip. "I'm sorry to be such a bother."

"You're not a bother," Trent assured her. "This will only take a minute."

Maybe she wasn't a bother to him but she was certainly getting on my nerves.

Trent followed me into the kitchen.

Paula assessed the situation with a glance, picked up a tray of cookies, and moved past us. "Excuse me. I'll just take these out front."

"Hang on a minute, Paula. Trent, is your ex-wife allergic to nuts?"

"Not that I know of."

"Then I guess there's no point in giving her a cookie with nuts. Never mind."

Paula disappeared through the door.

Trent scowled then grinned. "That was rude, but it was funny. Kathleen can try anybody's patience."

"Agreed." I took the key from my pocket and handed it to him. "Could this be the key her intruder was asking her about?" If there really was an intruder.

He accepted it, balanced it in the palm of his hand, and studied it for a long moment. "This is the key Jeff left for you?"

I nodded.

"And you're sure he didn't say anything about this while you were talking?"

"Oh, you mean some mysterious but meaningful message like, this is the key to the universe and the secret to happiness? No. Anyway, I already know chocolate is the key to the universe and the secret to happiness."

Trent nodded, took a small brown envelope from his jacket pocket and put the key inside. "I think you're probably right that Jeff was trying to get this key to me. I wish I'd returned his call. Maybe he'd have told me what it unlocks."

"Guess he thought since you're a detective, you could figure it out."

"Kathleen told the police she thinks the intruder is a friend of yours who believed she still had the key to my apartment."

"You didn't tell her about this key?"

"No. Is it possible Fred was trying to help you and went over there to scare her?"

I looked around the sink for a knife. All I saw was a butter knife. "That's not how Fred operates."

"We don't always know how Fred operates."

I moved closer to him, invading his space, and jabbed a finger at his chest. "You certainly know how I operate, and that does not include sending someone to that bimbo's hotel room in the middle of the night! Maybe she made up the whole thing. Maybe she killed Ransom to get that key. He didn't have it, so now she's trying to find out where it is." My theory had a few holes in it, but it had a nice ring.

"The intruder was real. Someone getting off the elevator saw a man dressed in black, wearing a ski mask come out of her room and run down the stairs."

I fisted my hands on my hips. "Was she also telling the truth when she said she still has the key to your apartment?"

"I told you last night she gave back my key. Kathleen doesn't always tell the truth. That little quirk of hers was one of the problems in our marriage."

"Little quirk? Seems like a pretty big quirk to me. Was she also lying about being back in your bed?"

He raked a hand through his hair and looked uncomfortable. That made me feel uncomfortable. "She was terrified after what happened. The officers who answered her 911 call stayed with her until I got there. I let her come home with me for the rest of the night." He looked me in the eye and stood straight, assuming his cop persona.

I stood straighter, assuming my red-head persona. "Terrified, was she? You just told me she's a pathological liar." Okay, that wasn't exactly what he said, but it was close enough.

"She's not a pathological liar."

"I can't believe you're defending her!"

His lips thinned. "You know there's nothing going on between me and her. When she's in my bed, I'm on the sofa. I shouldn't have to tell you that. I'd trust you if Rick was staying at your house."

I gave a snort of laughter. "You'd trust me not to kill Rick if he was staying at my house? Your trust would be misplaced. Is mine?"

Paula pushed through the door. "You need to come out here, Lindsay. Rick's here, and he and Kathleen are having a very friendly conversation."

Chapter Seven

And I thought the notion of Trent and me going to dinner with Rick and Robin was weird.

Rick and Kathleen together took weirdness to an all new level.

The two of them sat at the counter next to each other, smiling and talking, cups of Paula's coffee on the counter in front of them.

"Hi, Lindsay." Rick sparkled. He was *on.* "Kathleen and I were just talking about all the things we have in common. Being married to you two, of course, and I got to meet her husband yesterday." He patted her hand. "I'm sorry. Your deceased husband."

Kathleen lowered her gaze and nodded.

Yes, they had a lot in common, and being married to Trent and me wasn't even close to the top of the list. Being con artists topped that list.

Trent moved closer. "Mr. Kramer. I've been trying to get hold of you. We need to talk about your encounter with Jeff Gabler."

Rick chuckled. "Jeff Gabler. Your old friend and Kathleen's husband. Yes, that would be the man our Lindsay introduced as a convicted felon named Ransom. Such a sense of humor." He didn't look amused.

"If you have a few minutes, this would be the perfect time for you to come down to the station."

"Come down to the station?" Rick maintained his amiable expression but shook his head. "I'm not going down to your station. Kathleen and I are going to finish our conversation, and then I'm going to talk to Lindsay about a mutual business deal."

Trent's expression was also amiable. "No problem. If you can't come to my office, I'll go to yours."

Rick chuckled again. "That won't help you much since I'm not there."

"I'll wait. It'll give me a chance to talk to your co-workers."

Rick's amiable expression changed to one of horror. "You can't do that."

"Sure I can." Trent turned to me. "I'll call you later, Lindsay."

"Sounds good. I've got to get back to work." I headed for the kitchen door.

"Lindsay! I need to talk to you!" From the corner of my eye, I saw Rick slide off his stool. "It's important."

"Not as important as getting ready for the lunch crowd. I told you I'd call you when I got a chance, and I haven't had a chance yet. Go away!"

Rick grabbed my shoulder.

I spun around, trying to pull away from his grasp and incinerate him with fire from my eyes. Neither effort worked, but Trent jerked him backward, twisting Rick's arm behind his back.

"Did you just assault this woman in front of a police officer?" he demanded. "Lindsay, do you want to press charges?"

Trent was messing with Rick. I was pretty sure I couldn't really press charges for something so minor. But for a delicious moment I allowed myself to savor the thought. "No, I wouldn't want his son to suffer the stigma of having an ex-con for a father. Kid's already got enough to deal with."

Trent released Rick's arm with a flourish and stepped back.

Rick brushed his sleeve as if Trent might have left cop germs. "Lindsay and I have a business deal to discuss, if you don't mind, *officer*. A business deal involving chocolate. Right, Lindsay?"

I shuddered. How could I have considered even for an instant getting into business with Rick? Chocolate that passed anywhere near him would be tainted. "No, we don't. I'm quite happy with my chocolate sources."

I pushed through the swinging doors into the kitchen then stopped, far enough not to be seen but not so far I couldn't hear what was going on.

Paula looked up from chopping celery for chicken salad.

I put a finger to my lips.

"Kathleen, are you ready to go?" Trent asked.

Good, he was getting that woman out of my place.

Bad, he was taking that woman with him.

"Rick," that woman said, "please come with us to the station. I'd really like to hear about my husband's final hours."

Was she sucking up to Trent by getting Rick to give his statement or sucking up to Rick so they could get to know each other better?

Probably both.

I felt a twinge of jealousy at the thought of Trent and Kathleen together.

And I felt more than a twinge of fear at the thought of Rick and Kathleen together. They were sneaky and conniving without a shadow of a moral between the two of them. They could be dangerous.

"What was Rick talking about?" Paula asked. "What chocolate business?"

I reached into the pantry, took out a bag of chips, felt their weight in my hands, tilted one end of the bag up then down and felt the flow of the morsels inside. A comforting feeling. "Nothing. Rick claims to have a source of quality chocolate at a deep discount. Last night, for just the tiniest fraction of an instant, I thought about it."

Paula gave a distinctly unladylike *harrumph*. "Had you been drinking wine at Fred's?"

"Well, yes, a little." Her suggestion made me feel better. Being drunk was preferable to being stupid.

৶৵

After lunch rush was over, Paula and I were cleaning up when my phone played the first notes of *Out of a Blue Clear Sky*. Trent's ringtone. A burst of sunshine amidst the dirty dishes.

I set my tray on the counter beside the sink and answered.

"I detained Rick as long as I could," Trent said. "He wasn't happy when he left here."

"That's good. When Rick's happy, somebody else is unhappy. Did you get any information out of him?"

"His version of his encounter with Jeff Gabler differs a little from yours. He claims that he left after threatening Jeff with bodily harm should anything happen to you. Said that's why he was reluctant to come in, because he had threatened a man who was murdered."

"I'll bet he didn't agree to a lie detector test."

"I don't think it's going to come to that. He has an alibi and no motive."

"Bummer. I'd like to see him trying to con a lie detector."

"Kathleen seems to like him. I'm not sure that's a good thing."

I moved a couple of plates into the sink. "I'm pretty sure that's a bad thing. If the two of them pool their talents, we're all in danger."

Trent was silent for a long moment. He'd been doing a lot of that lately. "Kathleen's not perfect, but I can't imagine she'd get involved in any of Rick's shady deals."

I could feel the flames shooting from the top of my head again. "Did you just say my ex is worse than your ex?"

"No, of course not! Kathleen has her faults—"

"Yeah, like being a pathological liar and greedy and trying to make me jealous by telling me she's sleeping in your bed." That last part had worked, but

I wasn't going to let him know. "And she killed her husband for the insurance."

Another moment of silence. "I'm not even going to ask how you know about the insurance."

Oops. "It's what always happens on television." That wasn't a lie. I didn't say I saw it on television. "Thank you for verifying it. Does that mean you do have her on your suspect list?" I knew he wouldn't tell me, but I needed a diversion from the insurance thing.

It worked. Trent sighed. "I couldn't tell you if she was."

"If she's not a suspect, I guess she'll be going back to St. Louis soon. Get ready for the funeral and all that." I was torn between wanting her to have to stay in town because she was a suspect and wanting her to get out of town and away from Trent. I'd even volunteer to drive her all the way to St. Louis. Perfect chance to see if my driving really could give a passenger a heart attack. Lots of speculation but no proof.

"That's another reason I called," Trent said. "Jeff's memorial service will be in Pleasant Grove this Sunday. I thought you might want to come."

"Oh! Yes, I would like to. Kathleen's having the service here? What about their friends in St. Louis?" *What about getting her skinny butt back to St. Louis and out of this town?*

"It wasn't her decision. The attorney who's handling Jeff's estate called. Jeff left instructions that his memorial service was to be held here. Kathleen, Gary, and I are to work together to set it up."

"Oh," I repeated. "That's…" I wasn't sure what it was. Sentimental? Sad? Strange?

"I guess he wanted the four of us to be together one last time."

"Oh."

"I've got to get back to work. I'll let you know the details when Kathy and I get them worked out."

When Kathy and I get them worked out?

How cozy did that sound? He'd even returned to calling her by her old name.

"I'm sure Kathy will be thrilled about that."

"Gotta go. Love you."

"Love you too."

He'd already hung up.

I clenched my fists and leaned on the counter. Was I overreacting? I'd never been the jealous type, even when I discovered Rick was cheating on me. I hated him and I hated his women, but this emotion wasn't the same. This was painful and a little scary.

"What's *Kathy* going to be thrilled about?" Paula turned on the faucet and began rinsing dishes in the sink.

Using a great force of will, I unclenched my fists. "Seems Ransom left instructions for a big reunion at his funeral. Trent, Kathleen, and Gary. All the old gang, right here in Pleasant Grove. Working together. Trent's going to help *Kathy* with the details."

Paula opened the dishwasher and positioned a plate inside then reached for another. "That's interesting."

"Interesting? I think it's creepy." I clenched my fists again and slammed one on the counter. "He stole his best friend's wife. Now he wants the two of them to work together on his funeral? Is he trying to assuage his guilt by getting them back together? I thought Ransom was my friend!"

She paused with a wet plate in her hand. "Lindsay, you need to take a deep breath, drink a Coke, and eat some chocolate. I'm sure Ransom set up that request a long time before he met you, and, yes, he probably was feeling guilty when he did it. But you said their other friend, Gary, is included. So it'll be the three of them, not just Trent and, uh, *Kathy*."

"I hate it when you're logical. I liked it better when you called Kathleen a skank."

"She's still a skank."

"Thank you."

⇜❧⇝

We had just finished cleaning when my cell phone rang.

Fred.

"I was going to call you," I said. "I have new information."

"Tell me."

I told him about the memorial service to be hosted by Trent and *Kathy*.

"That might explain why Corey Paggett checked into the Pleasant Grove Manor this morning," he said. "He's an associate with Hoskins, Morris and Gabler. Jeff Gabler was his mentor."

"Ransom's friends are gathering to say good-bye." Suddenly the whole memorial thing became real. It wasn't about Trent and Kathleen spending time together. It was an occasion to bid farewell to someone who would be missed, someone I wished I'd had the opportunity to know better, someone who'd been murdered. If Kathleen killed her husband, she should be punished for ending his life, not just as a convenience for me to get her out of Trent's life, though that would be a pleasant side effect. "We need to talk to Corey Paggett. If he was close to Ransom, he may be able to tell us something about that key or maybe even that Ransom told him, *If anything happens to me, Kathleen did it.*"

"I scheduled an appointment for seven o'clock this evening."

"Great! Black suit? Lawyer garb?"

"Remember the red, purple, green, orange, and teal skirt you wore when you dressed as a hippie for a Halloween party?"

"Yes, I remember, but how do you know about it? I hadn't met you then. Have you got some kind of device that lets you see into the past?"

"You told me about the skirt a few months ago when we were preparing to visit Seventh Gate. At that time I deemed it inappropriate for the occasion. Tonight, it will be appropriate. Be at my house at six fifteen."

Having conveyed all the information he felt necessary, Fred hung up.

∂∽∾

73

That gave me time to go home, feed Henry, eat dinner, change clothes, make fresh cookies for Fred, and worry that Rick was going to show up before I got away. I hadn't had a chance to call him as I'd promised. Things had been busy at the restaurant, and I couldn't be expected to talk on a cell phone while I drove home. Trent was always telling me how dangerous that was, especially when I was talking to him while driving.

So Rick called me a few times…six or seven or ten or twelve. I quit counting after the second one.

Henry was off somewhere patrolling his territory when I walked through the gathering dusk to Fred's house. The evening shadows were cooler than the daytime sunlight, but I was comfortable in my hippie skirt, matching scarf, and peasant blouse. The outfit made me feel rebellious. I was intentionally a minute late. The time was sixteen minutes after six when I reached his porch.

He was ready. His 1968 white Mercedes waited in the driveway. It usually lives in his garage that stands upright at a ninety degree angle in contrast to mine which lists a little toward the southeast most of the time. When there's a strong north wind, it sometimes stands as straight as Fred's.

Fred greeted me at the door. He wore dark blue slacks with a gray blazer, a white shirt, and an ascot.

"An ascot? Seriously? I'm a hippie and you're going to the races?"

"You're late."

I handed him the cookies.

"Thank you. You're not very late." He took the cookies inside.

I strolled over to his car. He caught up to me and opened the door before I had a chance to touch the handle. Was he being polite or fearful I'd get fingerprints on his car?

Probably both.

We drove to the hotel in plush comfort, always going precisely the speed limit. Fred was capable of driving faster. The car was capable of going faster. Fred refused to go faster unless we were being chased by a crazy man in a monster truck.

"What's my name tonight?" I asked as he took a corner on all four wheels.

"Elizabeth Shelby."

Better than Abigail Sommers. Yes, he actually introduced me by that name during one of our field trips. "What's your name?"

"Walter Keats."

"Let me guess. We're poets."

"Close. I'm a teacher. You're my graduate assistant."

"Aren't I a little old to be a student, even a graduate assistant?"

He turned into the parking lot for the Pleasant Grove Manor. "You can be a non-traditional student, coming back to school after deciding on a career change, or you can be a professional student who has six hundred credit hours but doesn't want to graduate and be forced to go to work."

"Option one sounds better. I was formerly a stripper but now I'm going to be an English teacher."

Fred steered the car into the precise middle between the two lines of a parking spot. "No, you weren't a stripper."

"Okay, I was a prostitute. What's our story?"

"We don't have to discuss your former profession. We're doing an article about Jeff for our newsletter. We want our readers to see him through the eyes of the man he mentored."

We walked across the dimly lit lot to the ornate front door of the hotel.

The six-story Victorian style building was built in 1904 when the area was booming from the railroad that continued on to Kansas City. Now Pleasant Grove is a suburb of Kansas City and the main attraction...besides my chocolate...is the historical authenticity.

People in business or evening clothes moved about the high-ceilinged lobby, talking, smiling, frowning. Yesterday the lobby had probably been filled with policemen and yellow crime scene tape. Today it was business as usual.

The faint sound of piano music drifted from a bar on one side of the room. An arrangement of chairs and small tables filled the rest of that area. Fred pointed to a man sitting alone at one of those tables, a half-empty martini glass in front of him.

We started toward him, working our way through the maze of chairs, tables, and people. He rose and flashed unnaturally white teeth in the midst of his short beard. His dark hair was stylishly moussed and spiked. He wore a skin tight knit shirt tucked into skin tight jeans. He had nice muscles and a flat stomach, but somehow the way he stood as if posing for a picture made the package unattractive.

"Corey Paggett?" Fred asked.

"Yes, I'm Corey. You must be Doctor Keats."

He and Fred shook hands. "Pleased to meet you, Corey. Yes, I'm Walter Keats, Jeffrey's former professor and the creator of the Society of Poets and Pirates. Please call me Walter. There's no need to be formal when we shared a close friend." He released Corey's hand and gestured toward me. "This is Elizabeth Shelby, my graduate assistant."

Corey offered his hand to me. His smile became even wider, and his gaze raked over my fully clothed body as if it weren't. "You were friends with Jeff too?"

I nodded. "Yes. I was."

Corey's grip was strong. Usually I like that in a man, but somehow his cool, dry hand felt slimy.

I withdrew my hand and wiped it on my skirt.

"Please have a seat." Corey indicated the other chairs at the table. "Would you like a drink?" He waved toward a waitress crossing the room. "Honey, would you bring my friends a drink?"

Honey stopped and looked at us.

"Coke," I said.

"A glass of Pinot Grigio. The house brand will be fine." Fred's as picky about wine as he is about coffee. The house wine was likely only a prop to go with the ascot. I felt certain he had no intention of drinking it.

We sat.

Corey handed Fred a business card.

Fred handed Corey a business card.

Corey studied the card. "So you're an attorney as well as a college professor?"

Fred crossed his legs and looked nonchalant. There's nothing nonchalant about Fred. "That's the pirate part of the society. I'm licensed to practice in a few states, but I leave the hard work to you dedicated guys. Really sorry to hear about Jeffrey's death. I hope that won't have a bad effect on your career at the firm."

Corey shook his head. "The mentor thing was just a formality. I graduated in the top ten percent of my class. I'm in."

I wanted to ask if that class had been online from a third world country, but we were there to get information from the guy, not insult him. Maybe after we got the information I could do that.

The waitress brought my Coke and Fred's wine.

"Put it on my tab." Corey waved a hand and gave the waitress her share of his ultra-bright smile.

If I'd known that, I'd have ordered Dom Perignon.

"Jeffrey was an excellent poet." Fred lifted his glass and took a very small sip. "Did you read his work?"

Corey shook his head. "First I ever heard of him being a poet was when you called. His petitions and pleadings were pretty prosaic." He laughed at his own comment.

Fred laughed softly and insincerely. I took a drink of Coke. It was watery and flat, like Corey's attempt at humor.

Fred took a small pad and pen from inside his jacket. "May I quote you on that?"

Corey picked up his drink and draped an arm across the back of his chair. "You bet. What can I tell you about working with Jeff?"

Fred asked a couple of benign questions, and Corey answered with stories that always featured his own expertise. My mind drifted to more interesting things…whether the bulb in my bedside lamp was due to burn out soon, if the moon was waxing or waning, if Henry had enough catnip to get him through the week.

Fred leaned back.

I snapped to attention.

"Jeffrey had such a tough time with the drinking. You've only been with the firm a little over a year so you probably missed most of that."

"I interned there a couple of summers, but I didn't know about his problem until recently. He hid it well."

Fred nodded. "He was a strong man. He held it together even through the worst times. You know, a lot of creative people struggle with addictions. Look at Edgar Allan Poe, Tennessee Williams, Dylan Thomas, F. Scott Fitzgerald…" He paused and sighed. "It's as if we have to pay for the gift of talent. Elizabeth had her own struggle with alcoholism."

I don't know if Fred thinks he's training my ability to react quickly with startling revelations during our interviews or if he just makes this stuff up on the fly. I suspect the latter. I nodded gravely. At least, that was the expression I was trying for. Who knows if I looked grave or strange? "Just plain Coke now." I lifted my glass.

Corey gave me a cursory glance. He was more interested in telling his story than in my beverage choices. "Jeff couldn't have maintained much longer. People were starting to talk."

Fred arched a skeptical eyebrow. "They were? He got sober around a year ago."

Corey snorted, tossed down the rest of his drink, and held his empty glass aloft. "Honey, can you bring me another one?" He set the glass on the table. "That was his story, but he never quit."

Ransom had told me he hadn't had a drink in over a year. I'd just met the man. He had no reason to lie to me.

But neither did Corey.

"Why do you think that?" I asked. "Did you see him drunk?"

Another snort. "I didn't have to. Other people did."

I waited for him to provide details.

"Other attorneys at the firm?" Fred wasn't good at waiting.

Corey regarded Fred silently for a moment.

The waitress arrived, set a fresh drink on the table, and took his empty glass.

He sipped the new drink, set it carefully on the table, looked at me, then looked at Fred.

"When he was drunk, he liked to beat his wife."

I sucked in a quick breath. He had just corroborated Kathleen's story.

"Elizabeth, would you like another soda?" Fred's voice was untroubled.

"No. Thank you." I could have used a real Coke, one with fizz and flavor, but I didn't want any more of the hotel stuff.

"Did you see it happen?" Fred asked.

"I didn't have to. I saw the evidence. I saw the bruises. It wasn't the first time. Your sensitive poet was an abusive drunk."

I stared at Corey, at the tight shirt and spiked hair.

He *saw* the evidence? He *saw* Kathleen's bruises?

My imagination was running away with me. What I was thinking couldn't be right. Kathleen had been married to Trent then to Ransom. Two hot guys. She wouldn't…

"Did anyone else see the, uh, *evidence*?" I asked.

Corey shook his head and looked smug. "He was careful never to damage her face."

He was bragging about seeing Kathleen's bruises in places not exposed to the public.

I looked at Fred to see if he was thinking the same impossible thing I was thinking.

Fred refused to look at me.

He was thinking it too.

Corey and Kathleen?

Yuck!

Chapter Eight

"That woman killed Ransom!" I said as soon as we were in Fred's car with the door closed. "She killed her husband so she could collect the insurance and be with her disgusting lover."

Fred eased the car out of the parking lot and merged into traffic, a simple maneuver since the closest car was over two blocks away. "Not possible. She was with your boyfriend when he was killed."

"You know what I meant. She didn't do it with her own hands. She and Corey plotted together. He murdered Ransom while she established an unshakeable alibi with a cop."

"That is a logical possibility, but we need a little more evidence before we arrest the two of them."

"You can arrest them? I knew it! You're an undercover CIA agent!"

"I was being facetious."

He didn't deny that he was a CIA agent.

I stared into the darkness outside the windshield. "We'll get more evidence."

"Any thoughts on how we're going to do that?"

"You're the CIA agent. You come up with an idea."

"I'm still looking into that key. I'm quite certain it goes to a padlock, but the location of that padlock remains a mystery."

That was a first. Fred was having trouble finding something? "Have you checked…?"

"Yes?"

Where did one begin to look for a padlock? "I have no idea what the rest of that sentence was going to be."

"I've checked the local storage units and haven't found one in Ransom's name, though he could be using an alias if he really wanted to hide something."

"There's a storage unit facility just a couple of blocks from Death by Chocolate. Maybe Ransom had been there to leave something when he came to my place."

Fred turned onto our street. "I checked there first."

"Oh." I was disappointed my theory was wrong, but excited that my mind had begun to work like Fred's except a little slower. "Okay, so you've got that under control. I think our next step is to have a chat with Kathleen about her relationship with Corey."

Fred pulled into the exact middle of his driveway and stopped. "She'll come to us. To you, at least. Corey will brag to her about being the subject of an article in our nonexistent magazine. If he mentions your red hair, she'll know."

"I get it! If you'd wanted me to be disguised, you'd have made me wear a wig again. This way you're bringing her to us. You're brilliant!"

He didn't deny it.

He got out of the car, came around and opened my door. I sprang out and gave him a hug. He sort of hugged me back. A sort-of hug is a major expression of emotion for Fred.

I shivered as I crossed our yards to my house. The night air had a definite chill. A few fallen leaves littered both yards. Yesterday there had been a lot of leaves. Tonight Fred's elves would again clear every leaf from our lawns. He won't admit to having an entire staff of garden elves, but I'm not gullible. I know all that yard work doesn't happen by magic.

Henry trotted across the street to meet me. He had something in his mouth. In the dim light from the street lamp I couldn't be sure it was a mouse. I live in fear that someday he'll bring me one of Fred's elves.

We reached the porch and climbed the steps together. He laid a mouse at my feet.

Never thought I'd be happy to see a mouse.

"Thank you," I said. "I'm not hungry right now, but this will be a lovely snack for later."

He pretends to believe me when I say that.

I turned to wave at Fred. I couldn't see him but I knew he was there.

Henry and I went inside and I gave him his evening fix of catnip. While he was thus occupied, I went outside, put his gift into a plastic bag, and tossed it into the trash.

We climbed the stairs together and I put on my purple fleece pajamas. I love my hundred year old house…the authenticity, the wood floors, the ceiling moldings, the natural wood trim, the original windows with wavy glass and wooden frames that don't completely block the fresh air. That fresh air was getting colder every night. I had to compensate with something warmer than an old T-shirt.

A happily stoned Henry leapt onto the foot of my bed and began purring. The sound could be mistaken for a lawn mower. He's a big cat.

I turned off the light and settled under the covers. A warm bed, a happy cat. I was drifting into slumber within minutes.

Henry stopped purring, jumped off the bed, and streaked out the door.

My doorbell rang.

Damn.

It was only 8:30, but all my friends knew I went to bed early because I had to get up early.

Besides, Henry wouldn't react that way to a friend.

I climbed from my warm bed, slipped on the same moccasins I'd worn to visit Corey, and went downstairs.

Henry gave me a quick warning glance then returned to staring at the front door. All signs of catnip had disappeared from his gaze. He was sober and ready to repel the invaders.

The doorbell rang again.

I peered through the peephole but didn't turn on my porch light in case I wanted to pretend I wasn't home even though my car was parked in the driveway.

The roof of the porch shielded the figure from the street light, but I would have recognized that pale hair and those bulbous boobs in total darkness.

Kathleen.

I reached for the lever to release the deadbolt lock then paused.

A few minutes ago I'd been eager to see her, to question her and expose her guilt.

But I'd assumed Fred would be at that meeting.

If I opened the door, would I be letting a murderer into my house?

I looked down at Henry.

He had no answer for me. He continued to stand at rigid attention and stare at the door as if he could see through it.

I'd let a murderer into my house before. Paula's ex-husband.

But Fred had been hiding upstairs on that occasion.

However, he seemed to know everything that happened by using his telescopic x-ray vision and/or hidden cameras.

And this could be my opportunity to prove Trent's ex-wife was a vicious accessory to murder, not the weak, scared woman he believed her to be. If I could get her in jail, she wouldn't be able to whine herself back into his bed. And she'd probably look horrible in orange. Who doesn't?

I yanked open the door. "Good evening, Kathleen. What an unexpected pleasure."

Manners.

Okay, sarcasm. The two are often the same.

"I was in the neighborhood and thought I'd drop by. I didn't know you'd be in bed already."

"I'm no longer in bed." One would think that was obvious since I was standing in the doorway.

"Please come in." I flipped the light switch to turn on the lamps in the living room.

Henry gave me an *Are you crazy?* look, growled deep in his throat, and moved aside to allow her entrance.

With Fred spying on us and Henry in guard cat mode, I had nothing to fear from that woman.

"Thank you."

Should I lock the door so Corey couldn't come in and shoot me or leave it unlocked in case Fred needed to come in and rescue me?

Fred could break down the door if necessary.

I locked it.

"Please have a seat. Can I get you something to drink? Wine? Coke?" *A little antifreeze?*

"A glass of wine." She sat on one end of the sofa.

Henry stretched out on the other end and pretended to be a casual observer.

I went to the kitchen and took down two of my best mismatched wine glasses.

I have very high standards when it comes to chocolate. Not so much when it comes to wine.

I poured a couple of inches of white wine from a box into each glass then returned to the living room and handed the chipped one to her. It was just a small chip on the base of the stem. Not like she'd cut her lip drinking. Her finger, maybe.

That would not only be fun to watch, I'd have a sample of her DNA in case we needed it for evidence later.

I sat in my rose-colored recliner which, I thought, blended nicely with my purple fleece pajamas. Kathleen perched exactly in the middle of a large orange flower on the back of my sofa. I was right. The color didn't flatter her at all.

She sipped her wine, flinched, but smiled and crossed one slender leg with high-heeled black boot over the other. "You and I need to have a talk, woman to woman, about Adam."

I sipped my wine. It wasn't as good as Fred's, but it was better than the flat Coke I'd had at the Pleasant Grove Manor.

"What would you like to know about Trent?" I asked.

She blinked a couple of times. The breeze from her false eyelashes probably blew a few more leaves off the birch tree in my front yard. Might have even been strong enough to take a few off the oak. "Why do you call him by his last name?"

"Why do you call him by his first name?"

She hesitated and blinked again. More leaves for Fred's elves to dispose of. "It's what people do. Never mind. It doesn't matter. I haven't decided what to do about him yet. You still have a chance."

"Is that right?" What was she up to?

She had another sip of wine, uncrossed her legs and leaned forward.

I realized I was also leaning forward, waiting to hear what she had to say. I should have brought my cell phone and recorded the conversation. But Fred was probably getting every word on one of his devices.

I reversed my posture, crossed my pajama-clad legs and tried to look unconcerned.

Her eyes narrowed.

So did Henry's.

"Who's your tall friend with the white hair, glasses, and English accent?"

The *tall with white hair and glasses* part sounded familiar, but not the English accent. Fred's accent definitely wasn't Midwestern but I'd never considered it English.

Apparently Corey did.

I'd have to think about that.

"No idea what you're talking about." Yes, it was a lie, but she started it when she said she was in the neighborhood and just dropped by.

She set her chipped wine glass carefully on an unchipped portion of mosaic tiles on my vintage garage sale coffee table. "Corey's an idiot. When he bragged to me about being interviewed by the Society of Poets and Pirates, I knew somebody was sucking up to his giant ego. Jeff might have qualified for a pirate, but his poetry was lousy."

Interesting. Jeff had been a poet and Fred had known that. He might have even been a good poet. I trusted Kathleen's taste in poetry as much I trusted her honesty…slightly less than I trusted the man on TV who wanted to sell me the latest miracle gadget for only $19.99 then throw in another one *absolutely free, just pay postage and handling.*

"What do you consider good poetry?" I asked. "I've always liked T.S. Eliot and Ezra Pound. Maya Angelou, of course."

She gaped at me for a moment. Obviously she'd never heard of any of those people. She retrieved her glass and drained the contents.

I had her off balance. That was a good start.

"Also Edgar Allan Poe. Everybody knows *The Raven* but I think *Ulalume* is one of his best. We don't often hear about that one. What do you think?"

"What are you talking about?"

"Poetry and your husband. What kind of poetry did he write?"

"I have no idea and I don't care."

"Then let's change the subject and talk about something we both know, the identity of the man who killed your husband. Would you like another glass of wine?" Getting her drunk couldn't hurt. *In vino veritas.*

"No, I don't want any more wine." She curled her upper lip. "It's horrible."

"The more you drink, the better it gets."

I took her glass to the kitchen, refilled it, and set in on the table in front of her. She might not drink it. Or she might.

She folded her arms and glared at me. "Let's talk about the red-headed woman who was with the English guy, pumping Corey for information. I showed him a picture of you and he identified you as that woman."

Busted.

I looked at Henry. His gaze sent me a message. *Told you not to let her in.*

I needed to get back in control of the conversation.

I put my glass of wine on the table beside hers, lifted my chin, and folded my arms, imitating her aggressive posture. "Where did you get a picture of me?"

That stopped her momentarily.

"Why did Corey tell you about the interview?" I demanded.

She opened her mouth to speak but I was ready for her.

"Oh, that's right, because you're lovers. Yeah, he bragged about that. He's proud of having an affair with a hot chick. Those are his words, not mine."

Yes, it was another lie, but the cops lie to suspects, pretend they know more than they actually do, in order to get a confession. If they can do it, I can do it.

Her eyes narrowed to slits. She clenched her fists and breathed smoke and fire from her nose. Maybe not literally but she would have if she could have.

Fred would surely break down the door and rush in to save me before that happened.

I leaned closer. "You and Corey conspired to kill your husband and collect the insurance."

She shot to her feet.

I shot to mine.

Henry stretched and rose gracefully to his feet.

Fred must be waiting to get her full confession.

"You offered to share the insurance money," I accused, "if he'd kill your husband while you were at Trent's setting up an alibi." I shifted my balance to my left foot, ready to run. My legs were longer than hers and she had on those stiletto heels. I was pretty sure I could outrun her.

She reached down and snatched up her designer handbag. Damn! I couldn't outrun a bullet.

Henry snarled. The hair on his back bristled.

I shifted in the other direction in case I had to save my cat. He couldn't outrun a bullet either. Only Fred could do that.

She glared at me for a long moment. "You are one crazy bitch. You need to be careful or your mouth could get you in big trouble." She opened her purse and reached inside.

For a gun? For the knife Corey used to kill Ransom?

"You need to leave." I pointed a shaky arm toward the door. "The cops are on their way."

"I hope you're not a poker player. You don't know the first thing about bluffing." She withdrew her hand from her purse.

My heart slammed against my ribs.

She pointed the car keys at me.

Car keys surrounded by long red fingernails.

Not a gun or a knife.

My heart settled back into place.

"You keep messing with me, and I'll take Adam away from you so fast your head will spin."

Henry growled, the sound low and deep in his throat.

Kathleen looked at him then back to me, dismissing him as only a cat. "You don't have any idea who you're dealing with."

"Actually, I do, Kathy Ann Johnson."

The blood rushed to her face. It wasn't attractive against her red blouse. "You just sealed the deal. Adam is mine."

"Henry! Attack!" I commanded.

He hissed and bared his fangs.

She stepped away. "If that animal touches me, I'll sue you for everything you own."

She'd be pretty disappointed with that settlement. "Gonna use Corey for your lawyer?"

She strode across the room to the door and struggled for a moment with the deadbolt.

"Need some help?" I offered.

She got the door open and stalked out then slammed it behind her.

I followed, opened the front door and looked out in time to see her white Lexus speed away.

I grabbed my purse and keys from the table beside the door. I had to know where she was going.

I did not for one minute think she could take Trent away from me.

But maybe I thought about it for half a minute.

Long enough that I wanted to be sure she wasn't going to his apartment.

"Guard the place!" I yelled to Henry then ran through a cold drizzle to my car. That woman had a head start, but the slick roads might slow her down whereas I could handle them. My car may be old and dented with a few things that don't work, but it has great tires.

I sped after her, slid around the corner, and spotted a white car a couple of blocks ahead. Since it was the only white car…the only car…in the area, she was pretty easy to find.

I slowed. By that same logic, she'd be able to spot me. Besides, I didn't want a cop to pull me over and tell Trent I'd been speeding through the night in my purple pajamas.

She pulled onto the highway, and I breathed a sigh of relief. Trent lived on the other side of Pleasant Grove. She wasn't going to his place, but she wasn't heading for the hotel where she and Corey were both registered either.

I should turn around and go back home. Kathleen was from this area. She might be going to visit an old friend.

Nah. Women like Kathleen didn't have friends.

Maybe it was an old lover.

Or a new lover.

I'd come this far. I might as well see which exit she'd take off the freeway.

She drove a little over five miles then exited into an upper middle class residential area in Lee's Summit.

I followed.

She continued for a few blocks before she pulled into a driveway.

I eased up next to the curb a few houses away and turned off my lights.

She got out of the car and strode confidently to the front door.

A light went on and a man came to the door.

She went inside.

How many men was this woman sleeping with?

I drove slowly past the house and made note of the number. I'd have Fred find out who lived there and then I'd tell Trent. Yes, I was going to tattle on her. Somebody needed to.

I drove back home.

Fred was still awake. Light glowed through the blinds in his computer room. I could call him about the address.

I went inside, locked my front door, and started upstairs but hesitated on the first step.

I hadn't exactly got Kathleen to confess, but I'd upset her. People make mistakes when they're upset. They make bad decisions.

Like killing somebody who knows too much.

Maybe the man in the house was her partner instead of or in addition to Corey. Maybe she was even now telling him they had to get rid of me.

I got my iron skillet from the kitchen and went upstairs.

Henry curled at the foot of my bed, snoring softly.

I called Fred.

"I can't believe you went for a drive in your pajamas. I hope it was worth it."

Fred had been watching. I felt comforted. Or spied on. Whatever.

"She didn't go to Trent's place."

"Then she didn't spot you. If she'd known you were following her, she'd have gone there just to upset you."

I sank onto the edge of the bed and gave myself a mental slap upside the head. "You're right. She would have and I would have let her do it." Bright red anger flamed through my gut, anger at Kathleen and anger at myself that I would have allowed her to dupe me. "I have the address where she went. Can you get me a name?"

"Of course."

I recited the house and street number. "I'm going to take that woman down. She's going to jail and I'm going to visit her there and tell her how awful she looks in orange."

"That's beginning to look like a possibility. I have some new information. Carl Smith, a man who bears a striking resemblance to Corey Paggett, spent the last two nights at the Sleep-E-Z Motel a few miles from here."

"I was right! He came to town early to kill Ransom."

"Circumstantial evidence, but he had the opportunity. And checking into a motel under an alias is suspicious."

"How do you know Carl Smith is Corey Paggett?"

"Security camera. Go to bed and get some sleep. I'll call you tomorrow with a name for that address." He hung up before I could ask what made him look at the security camera footage in the first place. He'd just give me another oblique answer.

❧

Hoyt Axton burst into my dreams singing *Wild Bull Rider*.

I sat bolt upright in bed.

Fred's ring tone.

1:45 a.m.

I grabbed the phone. "Do you have another woman stuck in your closet?"

"No, but you have an ex-husband breaking into your restaurant."

Chapter Nine

Fred insisted on driving. This time he used the power I knew he had under the hood of that car.

"Way to go, Fred," I complimented as he turned a corner on two wheels.

A few minutes after we left his driveway, we pulled into the alley behind Death by Chocolate.

Rick and a tall stranger looked up at our arrival. Both men had boxes in their arms and had been moving toward my open back door until they saw us.

Boxes with the logos of well-known chocolate manufacturers.

Rick's chocolate scam. The one I'd almost been sucked into.

I leapt out of the car before Fred came to a complete stop. "What are you doing?" I demanded.

Rick smiled. "Hi, Lindsay!" He turned to the other guy. "It's okay, Clayton. Lindsay, this is Clayton Underwood, Robin's brother."

"Robin's brother? You involved Robin's brother in your scheme?" I tried to slam the car door. The Mercedes was too well built. It closed quietly. That added to my frustration. I strode over to Rick. "This is all so wrong I don't even know where to start!"

Rick nodded to Clayton. "Go on inside. I'll be right there."

Fred joined me. "I would be very interested to hear why you've broken into Lindsay's place to move boxes of chocolate inside. That's not the way a burglary usually works."

I balled my fists. "I don't care why! Just shoot him!" I didn't know if Fred had a gun with him, but Rick didn't know either.

Rick's smile wavered. Moisture glistened in his hair and on his face. I knew it was rain, not sweat, but it added to his guilty look. "Why don't we get the rest of these boxes inside before the rain damages the contents? Then we can talk."

In my anger, I hadn't noticed the seven other boxes sitting in the alley, all with stickers of various premium brands of chocolate, all getting wet.

My one moment of weakness, of agreeing to talk to him about the chocolate scheme, of not saying *No* over and over and over…it was enough for him to go ahead with his plans. In fairness to me, he'd probably have gone ahead with his plans even if I had said *No* over and over and over.

Clayton looked guilty as he came out, picked up another box, and went inside.

Rick followed.

"I'm calling the cops!" I yanked my cell phone out of my pocket.

Fred laid a hand over mine. "You may not want to do that."

I tried to free my hand. "I'm pretty sure I do."

"Clayton's been in trouble before."

I stopped trying to get control of my cell phone and looked at Fred's not-quite-serene profile. "What kind of trouble?"

"Drugs. A year ago when he was eighteen he was caught dealing meth. Robin hired a lawyer and got him off with two years' probation. If you report him to the police for breaking and entering, they'll revoke his probation."

Rick came out to get another box.

"I'm going to kill you," I promised him. "Not just for what you're doing to me but for what you're doing to Robin's brother."

He ignored me and carried the box inside.

I stalked into my kitchen. It was full of boxes, probably forty or fifty.

Clayton avoided my eyes as he went out to retrieve another one.

Rick started after him.

I grabbed his shoulder. "Get these boxes out of here! This is insane! There's no room for Paula and me to cook."

He shrugged off my hand. "No problem. Somebody will be here any minute to pick them up. When you didn't call me, I called you several times and left messages. You should check your voicemail more often." He tossed the last words over his shoulder as he went outside.

Of course this whole thing was my fault.

Fred came in. "Lindsay, it might be a good idea if you go home and let me handle this." He extended his car keys to me.

I gaped at him. "Go home? Drive your car? Are you having some kind of mental breakdown?"

"I'll call you to return for me when this is over."

I shivered and not because of the cold damp that trickled through the open door. If he wanted me to go home so badly he'd let me drive his car, something awful was coming down. "No." I wasn't about to miss that something awful.

Rick and Clayton moved the last of the boxes inside. Clayton went out and Rick closed the door behind him.

"Get him back in here," I ordered. "I want to yell at both of you."

"He's waiting for our partners to arrive."

Fred moved between Rick and the door. "Rick, you no longer have ownership in this piece of property. Breaking in was illegal."

Rick shrugged. "I had no choice. Lindsay wouldn't return my phone calls, and she changed the lock."

I clasped my head with both hands. "You had a choice! You could have stayed outside!"

"Not with the rain, babe. Cardboard boxes. No harm done. I didn't break down the door. I just used my little gadget to open the lock."

Great. He had a *little gadget*. Now I couldn't even lock him out. "After I told you I didn't want to get involved, why did you do it anyway? Why didn't you have this stuff delivered to your house or your office?"

"It's chocolate. We had to have a verified end user to get it into the country."

"*A verified end user?*" I looked around at all the boxes. "I use a lot of chocolate. I would not use this much chocolate in a year!"

"They don't know that."

A truck rumbled up outside.

Clayton opened the door. "They're here!"

Rick gave his brightest salesman's smile. "We'll have these boxes out of your restaurant in five minutes flat."

He and Clayton each grabbed one.

"Who are *they?*" I called after him. "Fred, who are *they?*"

He stared after Rick and shook his head.

I reached for a box. "Let's help them get these gone."

Fred restrained me. "Don't touch them."

I drew back my hand. I wasn't sure if Fred thought the boxes were toxic or that I shouldn't get my fingerprints on them. In either event, I decided to take his advice.

Rick and Clayton returned with two large hairy men. I would not have wanted to meet either of them in a dark alley.

The new guys carried two boxes at a time. The four men emptied my kitchen in a short time. Probably longer than Rick's promised five minutes, but not by a lot.

Clayton and the new guys left. Rick stopped just inside the door. "I'll see that you get free samples for your trouble, Lindsay." He smiled and winked.

"I don't want free samples!"

He closed the door, and I breathed a sigh of relief that the mess was over. "I've got just enough time to go home and shower before I have to come back for work. I'm going to be dragging tomorrow. Well, today, technically speaking."

"You'll be fine. Have an extra Coke or two." Fred strode toward the door then stopped and cursed. I wasn't sure I'd ever heard him curse before.

He flung the door open and charged outside. "Guys, you forgot one!"

He was right. They'd somehow missed a box sitting in the corner under the sink.

I cursed too, but that was no big deal. I've heard me curse a lot.

Rick came back in.

Fred pointed to the box.

Rick reached down and lifted it. The bottom fell out, dropping plastic bags of chocolate everywhere. He cursed too. Whole lot of cursing going on. "It got wet."

I grabbed a trash bag and handed it to him. "Use this. Just get your stuff out of here."

He held up a bag of dark cocoa. "Sure I can't tempt you?"

Of course it tempted me. That cocoa looked like the good stuff. "No. You have thirty seconds to clear out."

Fred stood threateningly beside the door. Well, he stood there casually, but somehow he looked threatening.

Rick cleared out with his trash bag of chocolate and the remnants of the soggy cardboard box.

Fred draped an arm around my shoulders. "I'll get you home as fast as I can so perhaps you can get a few minutes of sleep."

"Thanks." I had too much adrenalin pumping to be able to sleep, but I liked going fast in Fred's car so I didn't argue.

❧

I had a couple of extra Cokes the next morning and was my normal hyper self.

While Paula made biscuits, I put together my Chocolate Bundt Cake with Cream Cheese Filling. "We're going to have to get some kind of lock Rick can't pick and let himself inside any time he takes a notion to." I poured chocolate cake batter into half a dozen Bundt pans.

"Maybe a combination lock of some sort." Paula filled a large pan with biscuits. "That's pretty creepy that he just waltzed in here last night and brought in those boxes. If Fred hadn't called you, they'd have been in and out, and we'd never have even known it happened. How did Fred know he was breaking in?"

"After that crazy woman set fire to Death by Chocolate, he installed a security camera and an alarm. When the alarm went off in the middle of the night, he checked the camera and saw Rick." I added a portion of cream cheese filling to each pan then topped it with the rest of the chocolate cake mixture. "I wonder if Robin knows. If she does, surely she'd be worried about her brother and she'd shoot Rick. Maybe I should tell her."

Paula took two pans of cinnamon rolls out of the oven and put in the biscuits. "I don't think it would be a good idea for you to get involved in your ex-husband's relationship with his new girlfriend."

"But he's dragging her brother into something illegal!"

"Other than breaking in here, you don't know that what they're doing is illegal. You really need to stay out of it."

I slid my cakes into the other oven. I tried to slam the door. It closed with a *thunk* but not a very loud one. All of a sudden I couldn't seem to slam anything.

"Fine. Whatever. I won't call Robin and tattle on Rick. Sometimes you're not much fun."

She looked up and smiled. Of course she did. She won the argument.

"If new evidence comes to light, I reserve the right to change my mind," I said. "If Rick has sucked her brother into something that could get him thrown into jail and mess up his probation, she needs to know."

఼ఀఀ

Paula and I had scrubbed the last pot, put the last plate in the dishwasher, and cleaned the last tile on the floor.

Time to go home.

Finally.

I heaved a sigh of relief and went to double check that the front door was locked.

A man walked up to the door, lifted his hand in a wave, and smiled.

"Sorry, we're closed."

"You must be Lindsay."

My heart sank. The last time I heard that sentence was from Kathleen a couple of days ago and things hadn't worked out so well that time.

My phone burst into a piercing, annoying ringtone. Rick.

I considered not answering, but it gave me an excuse to turn away from the man at the door who insisted I must be Lindsay.

"Are you still at the shop?" Rick asked.

"We're just leaving."

"Can you stay a few minutes? I need to come over."

"No, we can't, and no, you don't." I hung up.

The man waited outside the door. He looked vaguely familiar though there was nothing outstanding about his appearance. Tall, brown hair, white shirt, gray slacks. Probably been in the place any number of times. I bit back the urge to tell him to go away. Maybe he wanted cookies for his elderly aunt who'd come to town unexpectedly. I couldn't afford to insult my customers. Being a minor celebrity carries a heavy burden.

I forced my tired lips to smile. "Can I help you?" I shouted to make sure he could hear me through the closed door.

"I'm Gary Durant. I went to school with Adam and Jeff."

"Oh!"

"I wanted to come by and meet you. Adam and I had dinner last night, and he told me all about you. I'm sorry I'm here so late. I got held up in court."

Rick called again.

I answered. "Go away!"

Gary looked startled.

I hit the *end* button on my phone. "Not you." I held up the phone. "Annoying salesman."

I unlocked the door and opened it enough we didn't have to shout. "Pleased to meet you, Gary." Yes, it was inane, but I couldn't think of anything else to say except *Go away*.

"Lindsay?" I turned at the sound of Paula's voice. She stood by the kitchen doors, handbag in hand, ready to leave.

"You can go on and pick up Zach. This is Gary Durant, a friend of Trent's."

Rick called again.

Paula didn't move.

I put the phone to my ear. "I'm on my way home already, Rick!" I hung up.

"I'll wait." Paula went back into the kitchen. She wouldn't go far. She has a very suspicious nature. She'd be listening.

Gary handed me a business card. "Again, I apologize for delaying you. When you have a minute, I'd like to visit since Adam said you talked to Jeff before he died. We lost touch, and I never got to say good-bye. I'd really like to hear about his last day."

My phone rang again. "I'm already home!" I shouted even as my sleepy brain registered that it had not been Rick's ringtone.

"No, you're not," Fred said.

"No, I'm not." I mouthed *Thank you* at Gary, locked the door, and turned away.

"I have a name for that address Kathleen went to last night."

A call from Rick beeped in. I ignored him.

"What's the name?"

"Gary Durant. He's—"

I spun around to face the door. Gary was gone. "No wonder he looked familiar. He was just here."

"What? Why?"

"Trent and Ransom's friend. Kathleen's sleeping with him too."

"You didn't watch the house all night to see when she left so you don't know that for sure. Why did he come to see you?"

I looked at the card in my hand. Gary Durant, Attorney at Law, Hoskins, Morris and Gabler. "Trent told him I talked to Ransom. Gary never got to say good-bye so he wanted to hear about his friend's last day. I can't wait to tell Trent that his ex is completing her round of sleeping with his friends. I wonder if she'll go after Lawson next. I'd like to see that." My nickname for Trent's partner, Gerald Lawson, is Granite Man. Not that I ever call him that to his face. But if I did, I doubt he'd register any emotion.

The thought of Kathleen going after him made me smile.

"Quite convenient that you have an invitation to talk to Gary. I'd like to go with you."

"Cool. He's already seen me, but you can be somebody fun. How about an undercover CIA agent? Or a famous racecar driver hiding from his fans?" I thought of Kathleen's comment about him having a

British accent. "How about my uncle on my mother's side who's just arrived from England?"

He didn't bite on any of my suspicions about him. "How about I'm your neighbor who's concerned about your welfare when meeting with a strange man while a murder investigation's going on around you?"

"Sounds a little boring but we can probably pull it off."

"You set up the meet and I'll be there." Conversation over. He hung up.

"Are you ready to leave?" Paula was as close to tapping her foot as I'd ever seen her.

"I'm very ready." I brought up voicemail as I walked through the kitchen doors.

The last time I'd ignored Rick had been a disaster. I needed to know what he was up to.

"Lindsay, this is important. When that box broke last night, we missed one of the bags of chocolate. I'm on my way over to get it."

I said a four letter word that would have got me sent to my room if I still lived at home.

Paula halted halfway out the back door. "What's wrong?"

"Rick lost a bag of chocolate and now he's coming over here to break in and dig around in our stuff looking for it." I called his number.

"Did you get my message?" he asked.

"Last night you offered me free samples. Now you've lost one bag. We'll call it my free sample. What's the big deal?"

"I didn't realize the people we're working with were so anal." He gave a short burst of phony laughter. "I'm coming by to get that bag."

"It's not here. You lost it somewhere else."

"I don't think so. I'm on my way to check."

"Do not come over here. I'm looking for it now." I laid the phone on the counter then got down on the floor in the area where the box had fallen apart. Paula handed me a pair of rubber gloves.

"Hey, we just cleaned, remember?"

"Those aren't for the floor. They're for the bag if you find it."

Paula's a little OCD.

I put on the gloves. "There it is, under the sink." I retrieved the plastic bag and stood up, holding it at arm's length. Somehow the contents didn't look so tempting anymore.

I picked up my cell phone. "Are you still there?"

"Of course."

"I found your bag."

"Thank goodness! I'll be right there."

"No! We're leaving. Now. Walking out the door. I'm taking the bag home with me."

"I'm heading for your house."

Rick at my house?

"I'm tired. I'm going straight to bed. I'll leave the bag on the swing on my front porch. Do not ring my doorbell. Do not knock on my door. Do not pick the lock. Do not come inside. Just take your bag and leave."

"Of course. Thank you!"

I hung up.

"I don't like the sound of this," Paula said.

"Neither do I. Why is he so eager to get hold of one bag of cocoa?" I hefted the object Rick found so desirable and studied it closely. "I have ten times this much cocoa of the same quality. What makes this particular bag so special?"

Chapter Ten

I dropped the bag of cocoa on my porch swing as soon as I got home.

Henry greeted me at the door and led me to his empty bowl in the kitchen. I fed him then let him out to patrol his territory.

Rick lives about twenty miles away and would have to drive through rush hour traffic. That gave me a little time before I needed to hide. I thought about having another Coke and relaxing, but I'd already had quite a few in my effort to stay awake. I probably didn't need any more caffeine if I planned to get caught up on my sleep. The afternoon was cool enough to justify a cup of hot chocolate. Of course, midday in August is cool enough to justify a cup of hot chocolate in my world.

I sat down on the sofa with a cup of cocoa and a book. As soon as Henry came back from his ramblings, I'd give him some catnip and we'd go up to bed.

The hot chocolate was warm and soothing, and the novel pulled me into the story, into a world of someone else's problems and away from mine.

I set my empty cup on the lamp table and leaned back. The print in the book blurred and I closed my eyes for just a minute.

Maybe more than a minute.

The sound of primitive jungle cat noises jolted me wide awake and upright in my chair.

Henry.

Probably meant Rick had arrived.

I could wait for the noise to subside and assume Rick either got his bag and escaped or Henry took him down, in which event I'd find only scattered remains on the porch.

Or I could go out and watch the fun.

I put down my book to go watch the fun.

My cell phone rang.

Rick.

I opened the door.

He stood on the porch steps, cell phone pressed to his ear, eyes wide, a sheen of sweat glistening on his face.

Henry stood in front of the swing, tail waving gracefully, hair along his back erect.

Both looked at me.

"Lindsay, I'm so glad you're here!" That came from Rick, not Henry.

Henry strolled casually over to stand beside me. I reached down to pet him.

"Are you scared of a sweet little kitty?" I taunted. "He's just protecting his property."

"That animal is possessed." Rick moved toward the swing, his gaze never leaving Henry who growled deep in his throat. He wouldn't attack until I gave him the command. Actually he wouldn't attack until he decided to, but if his decision coincided with my command, it would be great fun.

"Good afternoon, Rick." Fred strolled casually over to join us.

"Hi, Fred." The perspiration on Rick's face increased even though the evening was cool. He has the same opinion of Fred as he has of Henry. Possessed. Dangerous.

I picked up Henry and pointed to the swing. "Get your bag and go."

Rick moved toward the swing. "What the hell?"

I looked closer. Oops. Henry must have developed a sudden taste for chocolate. The plastic was shredded and the contents were spilling out.

I was torn between delight at Rick's distress and just a tiny bit of guilt that my cat had destroyed his property. Not really enough guilt to notice. "Don't freak out," I said. "I'll replace it. They'll never know. I've got some plastic bags and plenty of cocoa."

I set Henry on the porch and stepped over to the swing to retrieve the remnants.

Moving with the speed and stealth of a cat, Fred came up behind me and grabbed my arm. "Don't touch that."

Sometimes he goes a little overboard about germs. I suspect he showers wearing plastic gloves.

"Rick, what is that?" Fred pointed to a small white corner of plastic almost hidden by the mess of cocoa.

Rick swallowed. Actually, he gulped. "I don't know." The fear in his whispered words suggested he was lying.

I narrowed my gaze and scowled at him. "You do."

He stepped away from the swing, moving backward toward the steps. "I don't! I swear I don't!"

Fred took his arm, probably not as gently as he'd taken mine. "I don't think you should leave just now. Lindsay, would you please go inside and get a brush? I want to dust off the cocoa and see what's in that white bag."

I looked at Henry. He smiled and leapt off the porch into the yard. His work here was done. He could go play with the field mice and Fred's elves.

I brought Fred an old paint brush.

He carefully swept away the remnants of cocoa from the small bag of white powder.

I stared at it. "Rick, please tell me that bag contains baking powder."

He gulped again. "I don't know."

Fred's gaze was cold. "But you suspect."

Rick licked his lips and shook his head. "No, I don't. Maybe. I'm not sure." His normal cocky expression had changed to one of fear. "They got upset when they found we were a bag short. I even offered to go out and buy some cocoa to replace it, but they said they had to have that particular bag."

I lifted my hands and looked toward heaven for guidance. All I saw was the roof of my porch. It needed to be painted. "It's bad enough you got into something like this, but I cannot believe you got Robin's little brother involved! He's on probation! You're going to be responsible for sending him to prison. How do you think that's going to affect your relationship with her? My guess would be, not in a good way. What were you thinking?"

Rick smiled nervously. "The boy couldn't get a job. I was trying to help."

I clenched my fists to keep from hitting him. It would hurt my fists more than it would hurt him. "Help him? Not likely! It's all about the deal, the money. That's what you were thinking about! You're going to prison and so is Clayton. Robin is going to hate you, and I don't blame her!"

Rick lifted his chin and made an effort to retrieve his arrogant mien. He failed. Fear and arrogance don't mix well. "It was a business deal, that's all. A client rented space for a new restaurant in the River Market area. I told him about your place and how successful you were. He offered to cut me in on his chocolate supplier so you could benefit. I was thinking of you, and this is how you show your gratitude. I should have known better than to try to help you."

"Yeah, you were going to help me right into jail!"

"You never appreciate what I do for you!" He turned to leave, but Fred again took his arm.

"Lindsay," Fred said quietly, "please call Trent. Ask him to bring along an officer from drug enforcement."

"No, wait!" Rick struggled impotently to escape Fred's casual grasp. "I can fix this. You don't want to get the cops involved. We'll put this back together." He motioned toward the mess in my swing. "I'll give it to those guys and they'll be happy. The next time, I'll tell them I can't get involved. Problem solved."

"Lindsay, please call Trent."

I hit Trent's speed dial.

Trent answered.

"Lindsay," Rick pleaded, "you don't want to see me go to prison."

"Hey, Trent," I said, "we've got a drug dealer on my front porch with enough evidence to send him to prison for the rest of his life."

I was exaggerating Rick's potential prison sentence, but the terror on his face told me he believed it.

⊱⊰

We were still standing on the porch when Trent got there. Fred didn't want to leave Rick or *the evidence* alone. I suspected he was afraid Henry would return, shred the small packet, and get high. If he'd wanted to do that, he'd have already done it. Organic catnip is Henry's drug of choice, not some white powder.

Trent and a short, fierce looking guy came up the walk. He introduced the newcomer as Detective Ryan Morton.

"Lindsay," Trent said, "why don't you and Fred go inside and have a chocolate chip cookie?"

No hug, no kiss, no *Glad to see you.*

"Are you kidding? I don't want to miss this."

Fred took my arm again. "I'd really like to have a chocolate chip cookie."

"Traitor."

We went inside. I brought out the cookies and two glasses of box wine.

Fred took a bite of cookie but looked askance at the wine.

I sipped mine. "How did you get here?"

"I walked. You saw me."

"No, I mean, how did you know something was going on over here?"

"The entire neighborhood heard Henry. That cat has great vocal range."

I smiled proudly and drank more wine.

Fred took a sip of his and didn't make a face. He has impeccable manners.

Trent came in. He looked disheveled, angry, and tired. "Ryan's taking Rick to the station. They'll bring in Clayton and try to work out some kind of deal where the two of them will lead us to the suppliers and the people who were going to sell the drugs. Rick swears neither he nor Clayton knew it was anything other than a slightly shady deal with chocolate seconds."

I bit my lip and refrained from saying that Rick lies as easily and as often as other people breathe.

Fred stood. "I'm heading home since you have things under control, Trent. Thank you for the cookies, Lindsay." Even his impeccable manners did not extend to thanking me for the wine.

I walked him to the door and locked it behind him then got Trent a glass of wine.

He shook his head. "I have to drive home."

"Take it. You're going to need it."

"I already need it." He accepted the glass and sat on the sofa.

I settled into my chair across from him. "Your ex-wife is sleeping with your friend, Gary Durant."

He halted with his glass halfway to his mouth. "What?"

"I think she's on a mission to sleep with all your friends. You'd better warn Lawson."

"Why do you think she's sleeping with Gary?"

"She came here to yell at me last night and I followed her to his house."

I had his attention.

He took a drink of wine and frowned. My box wine or the news about his ex-wife? "Kathy came here? To your house? Why?"

I opened my mouth to tell him about Corey but realized if I did, I'd have to admit that Fred and I had talked to him. "She warned me she was going to take you away from me."

Tell me that would be impossible!

"That's crazy. She's just trying to cause trouble."

"Off the top of my head, I'd say she's succeeding."

"I'm going to warn her to stay away from you, and you need to stay away from her."

That wasn't exactly the response I'd been hoping for.

He rose and came over to me, pulled me to my feet and wrapped his arms around me. That was getting closer to the appropriate response.

The long, delicious kiss that followed took some of the sting from his order.

"Want me to stay a while?" he murmured against my hair.

"I hate to turn down an offer like that, but I'm totally exhausted. I didn't get much sleep last night."

He kissed the top of my head. "We'll make up for it this weekend."

I liked the sound of that.

We walked out onto the porch together, shared another kiss, and he left.

I opened the door to go back inside. Henry darted onto the porch and through the door.

"You better not be bringing a mouse or an elf into the house!" I shouted after him.

He ignored me and ran upstairs.

He was already in bed when I got there.

Good idea.

I was running through a jungle, tripping over vines and trees. A huge lion with Rick's features roared and screamed close behind me, nipping at my heels.

I turned and fired a gun at him.

The bullets melted in mid-air.

He kept coming, his horrible shrieks increasing in volume.

I ran as fast as I could…and woke with a gasp.

I was dreaming.

But the lion was real. I could hear him downstairs, screaming his horrible jungle sounds.

Henry.

Was Rick back?

I slid out of bed. I was going to kill him. Fred would help me hide the body.

I grabbed my cell phone and hit Fred's number as I raced downstairs.

The front door was closed.

The sounds were coming from the kitchen.

Rick must be at the back door, probably picking the lock with his little gadget.

I would beat him severely with my marble rolling pin before I killed him.

Fred answered the phone.

"Rick's here again! Bring the machine gun and be sure it's loaded!"

I charged into the kitchen.

Rick, clad in a black ski mask, black sweat shirt, and black pants, was trying to get out the back door while battling the half inch fangs and claws of my angry twenty-three pound cat.

I grabbed my rolling pin and held it aloft. "I'm going to kill you!"

He got out before I could whack him over the head.

Henry morphed into a house cat again. He looked me over carefully as if to be sure I was okay, licked his paws, and sauntered toward the stairs.

I surveyed the kitchen. Henry had done some damage. Bits of black were everywhere, some tinted with red. I smiled.

The back door opened and Fred stepped inside.

I frowned. "Where's your machine gun?"

"You appear to be unharmed."

I nodded. "I ran him off. You're barefoot. I'm flattered you came so fast you didn't even dress. Those are cool pajamas." White with a black belt. Pristine except for a red splotch on the wrist of one sleeve.

"These are not pajamas. This is my gi. I was doing a karate workout. And your intruder wasn't Rick. He's still down at the police station."

The intruder wasn't Rick.

I'd just threatened a stranger with my rolling pin. What if the man had a gun?

Fred once told me, *Never bring a rolling pin to a gun fight*.

"We need to catch him!" I started toward the door.

Fred held out a restraining arm, the one with red on the sleeve. "He's not going anywhere."

I gulped as I realized what that red stain might be. "You caught him? That was pretty fast, even for you."

"He appears to be dead."

"You—" I swallowed— "killed him?" I had often wondered if Fred was a black ops agent who killed when the government told him to. But that was all fantasy. I was shocked to think he had actually killed someone. And in my back yard.

"I didn't kill him. He was already dead when I came up. I checked for a pulse and didn't find one." He lifted the sleeve with the red stain. "Come out and verify that this man was your intruder. Then you should probably call Trent again."

Fred held the door. I walked through and halted on the top step.

A large man lay crumpled face down in the middle of my patio. That man wore a brown jacket and tan slacks, not a black sweatshirt or a ski mask.

Dark liquid puddled around his neck and stomach. A gun lay beside his outstretched arm.

"Did you change his clothes?" I asked hopefully.

"What? No. Are you saying this isn't your intruder?"

I shook my head. "No. The man in my house was wearing black."

Fred flipped on the porch light.

I flinched. In the light the dark liquid was red. I liked it better when it was black.

He pushed past me and stepped carefully around the body. "Someone stepped in the blood and left footprints leading in that direction." He pointed toward Paula's house.

I looked where he was pointing and saw no one in the open spaces. Everybody except me kept their back yards trimmed. Mine was the only one with bushes so thick Fred had often warned me "somebody could hide a dead body in there and you'd never know it." If only they'd hidden this one in those bushes.

Chapter Eleven

I called Trent. He said he'd alert the necessary people and that I should remain calm and touch nothing.

"I just chased a man out of my house with a rolling pin and found a dead body in my back yard. I am not calm, but I can promise you I won't touch anything except maybe a can of Coke."

I called my closest neighbors, Paula and Sophie, to let them know what was going on so they wouldn't worry. "Just an anonymous dead body," I assured each of them. "Nobody we know."

They both asked to speak to Fred. I could understand Sophie wanting to chat with him. She may be having an intimate relationship with him. But my reassurance should have been enough for Paula. After the last couple of years, surely she knew I could handle dead bodies with almost as much expertise as making chocolate chip cookies.

Then we waited. Fred and I were both barefoot but he didn't seem to mind the chill. My toes were taking on the color of my pajamas.

"Ever walk over hot coals?" I asked.

He scowled. "That's a strange question, even for you."

"Your feet seem to be impervious to cold. I thought they might also be impervious to fire."

The first emergency vehicle screamed down the street with lights flashing, effectively ending our conversation about feet.

"They're here," I said.

"I noticed."

"We'd better go talk to them."

"You go. I'll stay with the body."

"He's not going anywhere."

"You've become quite adept at stating the obvious tonight."

"Yeah, okay. I'll send them back here." I would have preferred that Fred go with me, but I was eager to get away from the dead man.

I went to the front yard and directed first the EMTs then the other arrivals to the back where Fred and John Doe waited.

Within ten minutes various members of the Pleasant Grove police and fire departments were milling around all over my yard. Every emergency vehicle they owned, all five of them, flashed bright colors up and down the street.

Lights came on in neighboring houses. Doors and windows opened. People in robes and slippers came out on their porches to see what was going on. I was hosting another middle of the night block party and once again I was without cookies to serve the guests. Fortunately, no one left their porch and came close enough to notice my hostess deficits.

Gerald Lawson got out of a dark sedan and crossed the yard toward me. The multi-colored lights danced across his steel gray hair in flamboyant contrast to his stern expression.

Odd that he arrived before Trent when I'd called Trent first and assumed he'd rush to the side of his freaked out beloved.

A vivid green demon inside my brain whispered that perhaps he was already at the side of his beloved.

Lawson approached. "You okay?"

I shook my head. "Where's Trent?"

"He'll be here soon. Let's go see what you've got this time."

It was as close to comforting as Lawson got.

He and I trekked through the cold, damp grass to the scene of the crime. Lawson was wearing shoes. He probably didn't know the grass was cold and damp.

People in uniforms hovered around a central location, taking pictures, putting things into tiny bags, and talking in words of at least five syllables.

Fred greeted Lawson with a handshake as if this were a business meeting or something normal.

"Fred found the body," I said, trying to shift the focus from me.

"In your back yard," Lawson said.

"I found a dead squirrel in my front yard last week. You going to blame me for that one too?"

Both men looked at me strangely.

Lawson took out his little notebook. "So you found the body, Mr. Sommers?"

"I'm going inside to get some shoes," I said. "My feet are freezing."

No one objected so I went inside my warm, secure home.

Damn.

Finding a body had taken over my brain. I'd momentarily forgotten about the black and red chaos created by Henry. This would doubtless be considered part of the crime scene. I thought about the time Rick's car had blown up in his driveway with Rick's woman of the week inside. His house had been closed off for several days with that ugly crime scene tape. I didn't want to be locked out of my house.

On the other hand, I wanted the intruder/murderer caught.

Suddenly my feet weren't the only cold part of me. A sliver of ice slipped inside my chest.

An intruder wearing black.

The same intruder who'd broken into Kathleen's hotel room?

Kathleen claimed the alleged intruder had been looking for a key. She told him she gave the key to me.

Now someone had broken into my house.

Had he been looking for the key Ransom left me?

If Henry hadn't stopped him, would he have come upstairs and demanded I give him that key?

What could it possibly unlock that was so important someone would break into two places to get it?

My mouth was suddenly as dry as a cookie forgotten in the oven for half an hour.

Not only had someone broken into my house, he'd murdered a man outside my house. The action had ramped up.

Ransom's hotel room had been searched when he was killed. Was his murderer looking for that key?

Ransom had thought something was important enough it had to be locked away.

From his wife?

She thought the man who came to her room demanding a key was talking about the key to Trent's apartment. If she was genuinely confused, that meant she knew nothing about the key or the man trying to find it.

That still didn't mean she was innocent of setting up her husband's murder.

I hurried upstairs and changed into jeans and a sweatshirt as well as wool socks and boots.

Henry opened one eye then rolled over and went back to sleep. He'd had a tough night protecting his home.

So had I.

I went downstairs and out the back door.

The crowd was still there.

The body was still there.

Fred saw me. "We need to come inside," he said. "See if your intruder left any evidence."

"He did."

Fred and Lawson entered.

"Your kitchen's a mess," Lawson said.

I straightened my shoulders and lifted my chin. "That's the evidence. My cat took some DNA samples from the guy who was in my house. You can thank him later."

"We're going to have to get the forensic guys in here. You should probably leave the premises while we do that."

Fred nodded. "Let's go to my place and have some hot chocolate."

"Sounds good, but I need to get Henry."

Fred shuddered. He considers Henry a walking hair dispersal system. "Why? He doesn't like hot chocolate."

"Yeah, but he likes to attack strangers who come into my house." I looked through the window at the people milling around in my yard. "Your forensic guys are strangers to him."

"You can't take your cat," Lawson said. "He may have more evidence under his claws."

"And you're going to collect that evidence?" I snorted. "Good luck. Unless you want to deal with Henry's Mr. Hyde persona, you should let me hold him while you do it."

"Your cat's always been friendly when I've been around him."

"That's because Trent's always been around at the same time. He likes Trent. Why isn't Trent here?"

"I don't know." Lawson headed back outside toward the lights and party.

Really? I'd asked the tough question, put myself out there, and all he could say was *I don't know*?

Fred took my arm. "Come with me. You might not be able to find your way to my place alone."

"I think I can find my way across our yards," I protested. "There aren't a lot of turns to confuse me."

"There's no point in taking any risks."

"Risks? You seriously think I might get lost?"

"No."

I gulped. "Oh. You think there's a chance the man in black…" I couldn't finish the sentence.

We went to his house. He brought me hot chocolate. I wrapped my hands around the warm cup and settled back on his sofa. I would have really liked to just lie back and relax. Let the comfort and security surround me. But I couldn't until I'd settled a couple of things.

"The intruder, the guy in black," I said, "he could be the same man who broke into Kathleen's hotel room looking for that key."

Fred settled in his recliner. "The thought occurred to me. If she really did tell that man she'd given the key to you, he could have come looking for you. If the man wants that key, he must know what it unlocks. This begs the question, if the key fits a padlock and this mysterious person wants whatever it guards, why doesn't he simply cut off the padlock?"

I shook my head and tried to focus my sleep-deprived brain on the question. "I give up. Why doesn't he?"

"It could be in some public place where he doesn't dare cut it off. We have to assume he knows where the lock is located. Otherwise, possessing the key wouldn't do him any good."

"Henry took samples of his DNA. Maybe we can track him down and torture the information out of him. What about the dead guy? Do we know who he is?"

"No one of my acquaintance."

"Don't evade my question. You had plenty of time to go through his pockets and search for identification before anybody official got there."

He set his cup on the coffee table. "He had no identification on him."

"That brings up a whole new set of questions. We need answers, not more questions. How was he killed?"

"He was stabbed and his throat was slit."

I licked my dry lips. "That's how Ransom was killed."

He nodded. "The victim had a gun, but it appears he got into a scuffle with your intruder and never had a chance to fire. My guess would be that the dead man was hiding in that jungle in your back yard, and the intruder came through behind him."

I shivered. The same man I'd pursued with a rolling pin had murdered a man in my back yard. "Did you get his fingerprints so we can identify him?"

"I didn't have my fingerprint kit with me."

"You've got enough blood on your pajamas to do a DNA test."

He looked at the red stain on the end of his white sleeve. I was surprised the force of his gaze didn't bleach it as white as the rest of his garment. "I doubt we need to do that. I'm sure the police will have an identity soon."

"Okay, so we'll just wait for the cops to identify him and you can hack into their database and find out who he is."

"Or we could watch the evening news report. You should finish your chocolate then stretch out on the sofa and try to get some sleep. I'll bring you blankets and a pillow."

Sleep beckoned, but there was one more question I had to ask. "Do you know where Trent is?"

"No."

"I guess this means you didn't put that bug in his apartment."

He left the room and returned with two soft blankets and a pillow.

Hot chocolate and a warm bed. I didn't reprimand him for not bugging Trent's apartment.

తొ<del></del>

I must have dozed off. I woke to the feeling of soft lips on my forehead.

I knew those lips.

I opened my eyes a slit.

In the pale glow of the lamp, Trent smiled a pale smile. "Good morning."

I laid a hand across my eyes and groaned. "Is it time to get up already?"

"I'm afraid so."

I looked at my watch and groaned again then sat up, yawned, and pushed back the blanket. "Yeah, it's almost time for me to go to work."

My eyes adjusted to the light and I saw a red scratch on Trent's cheek.

I was suddenly wide awake.

Had Kathleen with her long red nails given him that scratch?

In passion or anger?

Was she the reason he'd arrived late?

"What happened to your face?"

He lifted a hand to the affected area and grimaced. "Your cat didn't like having his nails scraped for DNA."

"Oh, good. I mean, it's good that you scraped his nails for DNA, not that he scratched you." What I really meant was that it was good Henry had made the scratch, not Kathleen.

"He took down a couple of the guys before I got there. Lawson's hands look like he got in a battle with a meat grinder and lost."

"I told him he should let me hold Henry." I was sorry he'd hurt Lawson and whoever else had tried to hold him, but I was also secretly proud of my cat. He'd stood up to men who weighed ten times what he did. I'd give him some extra tuna when I got home.

I staggered to my feet and yawned again. "I need to tell Fred I'm leaving."

"Good night, Lindsay." Fred's voice came from out of the darkness beyond the lamp.

Trent took my hand. "He let me in. Did you think I broke in?"

"Maybe. Good night, Fred. Thanks for the hot chocolate and the blanket."

Trent and I went from the lamp light in Fred's home to the total darkness of pre-dawn.

"Why were you so late getting over here?" I asked.

"Let's talk about it when we get to your place."

Not a good sign that he didn't want to answer my question until we got to my place.

I took a couple more steps and stopped on the brown grass area. "Okay, we're on my property now. Let's talk."

I've seen cops on TV make suspects talk when they didn't want to. I'm sure Trent's done his share of that. But I've never seen a TV show about a chocolatier forcing a cop to talk when he didn't want to. That morning was no exception.

We continued to my house in silence. Trent unlocked the front door.

I'd given him a key to my house because I loved and trusted him.

He'd given Kathleen a key to his apartment.

I chose not to finish that thought.

As soon as Trent pushed the door open, Henry charged out, glared at both Trent and me, and disappeared into the darkness.

He'd be back before I left for work. He knew where the food in his bowl came from.

We went inside. When the cops had searched Rick's house, they'd left things tossed around carelessly and fingerprint powder everywhere. "Looks better than when I left it."

"I made the boys clean up. There are a few benefits to dating a cop." He moved over to the sofa and sat, patting the cushion beside him. "Come sit down. We need to talk."

I edged toward the kitchen, trying to delay the inevitable. "Want me to make you a cup of coffee?"

He laughed and shook his head. "No, thank you. The night's been bad enough already."

"How about a Coke?"

"Thanks. A Coke would taste good right now. You'd better have one too."

I did not like the sound of that at all. He was going to tell me something so bad I needed a Coke to deal with it.

That nasty green monster, jealousy, niggled around the edges of my brain again.

Okay, it was doing more than niggling. It was eating away at me. This was an ugly feeling made up of hurt and betrayal and anger and the fear of loss, of not having Trent in my life. Now all those country songs made sense. Now I understood why wives killed their cheating husbands.

I didn't like the feeling one little bit.

I took my time getting our Cokes before heading back to the living room.

I was pretty sure I didn't want to hear what Trent had to say. If he told me he'd been with Kathleen when I called, I would hold my head high and deal with it…while baking cyanide cupcakes for the both of them.

I handed Trent his can, sat down beside him and popped the top on my Coke. A long drink of the fizzy, refreshing beverage made me feel half awake which was better than half asleep.

He took my hand and looked solemn. "We identified the dead man in your back yard."

"What? The dead man… This isn't about…?" I stopped myself before I said that woman's name. "You identified him. Good. I hate it when strangers drop dead in my back yard. Who was he?" I would have some information before Fred. I'd be able to tell him something for a change.

Unless he'd already discovered it while I was asleep.

"His name was Leon Scranton."

I shrugged. "I don't know him. Should I?"

"No. He's a drug dealer."

Suddenly I knew where this was going. I wasn't sure how we were getting there, but the destination was Rick.

"After you called, I went down to the station to talk to Rick."

He hadn't spent that time with Kathleen. Relief surged through me and drowned that jealous creature even as anger at Rick clenched my teeth. "Go on."

"We cut a deal with Rick and Clayton. They both claim they didn't know anything about drugs hidden in the chocolate. In exchange for them leading us to the dealers, they get no jail time."

"I'm glad Clayton won't go to jail, but are you sure you can't get Rick for something? Maybe for being obnoxious?"

He grinned wryly. "If I could do that, we wouldn't have enough room in our jails for all the prisoners."

"That guy, the dead one, came here looking for the missing drugs, didn't he?"

"It's possible. We had to buy some time to get the bag set up to look exactly like the original one. Rick was supposed to convince the men that you'd left the bag at the restaurant, changed the locks, added an alarm system, and he couldn't get in until tomorrow morning when you open. Rick put them off, and Ryan said it sounded like he did a good job."

"He's the quintessential salesman."

"Rick made the deal to deliver the package in the morning. They weren't happy about it, but they agreed. Ryan went over the details of the sting with Rick and Clayton, the wires they'll wear, what they need to say and not say, how to get the information without giving anything away. They were getting ready to leave when I showed up."

"So the man in black wasn't looking for the key? He was looking for drugs?"

"The key?"

"The key I gave you that Ransom left. The key Kathleen's intruder was looking for."

He shook his head. "We think the dead man was supposed to be the lookout while the guy in the mask came inside to find the package or to persuade you to hand it over. Since he was disguised, we assume he expected to be seen which meant a confrontation with you."

The intrusion wasn't about the key? Had Kathleen had been lying about what her intruder said? Could the man have been her accomplice, playing out a role in a scenario designed to get her back into Trent's apartment?

Too many questions. Nothing made sense.

"Lindsay? Are you okay?"

"Oh, yeah, sure. Sorry. I was just thinking. So if the two guys came here together, why did the man in black kill his buddy?"

"We don't know."

137

"Why did they come here instead of the shop where Rick told them the drugs were?"

Trent lifted a hand to his forehead and rubbed it. "We don't know. We checked your restaurant to see if they'd gone there first, but everything looks okay. No sign of a break-in."

"You're sure Rick told them the drugs were in the restaurant, not at my house? He's sneaky."

"Ryan was there the whole time."

"What happens with the sting? Is it off? Is Rick going to prison?"

"I'm sorry, no. They've got to go through with the sting, pretend they don't know anything about what happened here. We don't have any proof this was related to the drugs."

I spread my hands in frustration. "So you think a drug dealer and a murderer came to my house tonight by chance?"

"We don't know anything for sure yet."

"Maybe it was about the key instead of the drugs. Maybe the man in black was here to find it, and the dead guy was his buddy who just happened to be a drug dealer." That didn't sound right, even to someone with a big sleep deficit. "Okay, maybe he wasn't his friend since he killed him. Unless there's a third man involved." I sighed. "I'm going to shut up. This is getting sillier and sillier the longer I talk."

"Why would someone think you have the key?"

"Because your idiot ex-wife told the man...assuming there really was a man...that she'd given the key to me."

"Why would she say that?"

"Didn't she tell you she thought the intruder was a friend of mine, trying to get the key to your apartment?"

"Yes."

"So she told him I had it. To get rid of him, I guess. Who knows what that woman's going to do or why she does it?" As the words came out of my mouth, I thought maybe I shouldn't have been so harsh. This was a woman Trent had loved enough to marry. But I'd married Rick, and I didn't care what bad things Trent or anyone else said about him. They couldn't compare with the bad things I said. Nevertheless, I hurried on to change the subject. "Have you figured out what the key goes to yet?"

"No, and we don't know for sure that it had anything to do with Jeff's murder."

"He saw his murderer on the sidewalk outside my restaurant. He came back and left the key so that man couldn't find it and I could give it to you. It has to be a clue."

"That's one possibility."

"What other possibilities do you have?"

He gave me a quick kiss in lieu of answering. "Go get ready for work. You've got a big day ahead making sure everybody gets their chocolate fix, and I'm going to go home to get a couple of hours of sleep. Gary and I are meeting Jeff's parents this morning to plan the memorial service."

"Just you and Gary? I thought Kathleen was supposed to be included in the planning."

"Kathy and her in-laws aren't close."

"Does that mean they threatened to shoot her if she came down their driveway?"

"Not quite that bad, but we all agreed it would be best if Gary and I talk to Mr. and Mrs. Gabler then take the ideas to Kathy."

It was cute that he called them Mr. and Mrs. Gabler as if he were still a little boy playing with their son. "Did you stay in touch with them?"

"The day I told them about Jeff's death was the first time I've talked to them since Jeff and Kathy got married."

"But you were close before that?" Getting information out of him was like getting that first piece of chocolate pie out of the pan in one piece.

"Yeah. I spent almost as much time at their house as I did at my own. But then I grew up and left home and my folks moved out of the neighborhood. Then Kathy…" He shrugged. "Life changes."

"Guess this wasn't the best way to renew old acquaintances."

"They're good people. When this is over, they want to meet you. We'll have dinner with them and my parents."

They want to meet you. That meant he'd told them about me. They wanted to meet me, but they didn't want to be around their daughter-in-law. That thought made me smile.

I'd only met Trent's parents once, but I liked them and they seemed to like me. I brought them chocolate chip cookies. How could they not like me?

"See you tonight?" I asked.

"Tonight, all night. Somebody broke in here and somebody was murdered in your back yard. It doesn't matter if they were looking for drugs or a key or your collection of diamond jewelry which, I happen to know, isn't very large. I'm spending every night right here with you until we get this figured out."

I smiled again. If he was spending his nights with me, he wouldn't be spending them with Kathleen. "If I'm asleep when you get here, feel free to wake me up."

He wrapped his arms around me and held me close. "I won't be late. Lawson's taking the lead on Jeff's murder and your intruder since I have a personal involvement in both cases. He'll get stuck with all the overtime."

"Aren't you worried he won't do as good a job as you would because he doesn't have a personal involvement?"

He laughed softly, his breath warm on my neck. "Cops don't usually have a personal involvement with criminals."

I never thought I'd feel torn about Trent spending more time with me. I wanted him there, of course. But I wanted to solve Ransom's murder and put Kathleen in jail too.

Fred and I would have to redouble our efforts and work faster during the time we had in the evenings before Trent got to my house.

Chapter Twelve

Paula was sprinkling cinnamon and sugar on her dough when I dragged my tired body into Death by Chocolate that morning.

"What happened last night?" she asked without looking up. "Since you said it was an anonymous body, I assume you didn't kill Rick."

I tied on an apron and told her the whole story while I measured the dry ingredients for brownies. Well, the whole story except for my worries about Trent and Kathleen. That part wasn't essential to understanding what happened.

She rolled up the dough and began slicing. "That doesn't make sense. If the two men came to your house together, why did one of them kill the other?"

"I don't know. Trent doesn't know. But remember, Rick was involved, so it's normal for things not to make sense." I measured flour into my bowl and added cocoa.

"You do realize Rick and Clayton are going into something that could be dangerous. Rick's too cocky for his own good, and Clayton's just a boy, probably a scared boy."

"The cops will be there to step in if things go bad."

"It depends on how fast things go bad. I wonder if Robin has any idea about what her brother's involved in."

"I doubt it or she'd be performing brain surgery on Rick without any anesthetic." I stirred oil, butter and eggs in a separate bowl. "I'd like to see that."

"It may be time to tell her."

I was surprised that Paula had reversed her previous opinion and was actually suggesting I interfere, but I was even more surprised that I didn't want to. Yesterday I'd been thinking solely about warning Robin that Rick was a jerk and could be leading her brother into trouble. Today I'd have to tell Robin her brother was in big trouble. It no longer sounded like a fun thing to do. "That's not what you said yesterday. You said it wasn't a good idea for me to get involved in my ex-husband's relationship with his new girlfriend."

"Yesterday we didn't know this involved drugs and her brother was going into a dangerous situation."

I poured my brownie batter into three pans and put them in the oven. "I'll call her after we close." Put it off as long as possible.

"You don't think you should do it *before* her brother walks into danger?"

"Maybe." I washed my mixing bowl and prepared to make chocolate chip cookies. "Probably. But I don't know exactly when the sting is going down."

"Then call her right now."

"I have flour on my hands."

143

"Wash them."

I sighed, washed my hands, and took out my cell phone. Yes, I had my ex's girl friend's number. Not because I'm nosy or anything like that. She's a doctor. It's always a good idea to have the home phone number of a doctor handy in case something happens, like Rick getting a head injury from my iron skillet.

I sighed again, this time in relief when my call went straight to voicemail. I wouldn't have to deliver the news in person. I left a message detailing the entire situation, enough information she didn't need to call me back. But I ended with, "Call me if you have any questions." *Please don't have any questions! Just kill Rick and leave me out of it*!

The morning went by fast. I chugged a few Cokes and kept moving. I was surprisingly awake and alert. Of course, the adrenalin from finding an intruder in my home, a body in my back yard, and the worry that Robin would call me at any minute contributed to staying wide awake.

The lunch rush started winding down. I set a tray of dirty dishes in the sink and turned to go back and serve more chocolate. Paula came into the kitchen. "The couple in the far corner would like to talk to you when you have time."

Normally when someone asked to speak to me, they wanted to compliment a dessert or inquire about the recipe. But nothing was normal anymore. "What about?"

She looked at me solemnly.

My chest clenched. What kind of trouble was I in now?

"It's Ransom's parents."

"Oh." I went back into the restaurant area, to the counter, and glanced at the couple in the corner. They saw me looking and smiled. The woman gave a small wave. She was short with salt and pepper hair and a sweet smile. The man was tall, like his son, but thinner. They looked like nice people, the kind of people who could have raised a son like Ransom.

I waved back and gave them a thumbs up.

They were just starting on their Chocolate Caramel Peanut Butter Cake. They'd be occupied for a while.

I served dessert to a few more people then went to their table with a fresh pot of coffee. "Hi. I'm Lindsay."

The man extended his hand. Other than having streaks of gray in his hair, he looked very much like Ransom.

"Pleased to meet you, Lindsay. I'm Warren Gabler. This is my wife, Maggie."

I shook his hand then Maggie's. The laugh lines around her eyes told me she didn't usually look so sad. "It's very nice to meet Rans—uh, Jeff's parents. I only met him the one time, but we bonded over chocolate."

Maggie's eyes misted. "He did love chocolate. I hope you don't mind our stopping by. Adam and Gary came over this morning to make plans for..." She blinked. Her husband laid his hand over hers. "For our son's memorial service. Adam told us about

145

you and about Jeff's visit here. We just wanted to meet you."

"I'm glad you did. Trent—Adam—said we were all going to get together when everything is…uh…over." *Over?* I flinched at my own word choice. *When your son's funeral is over. When your son's murder investigation is over.*

Maggie wrapped a hand around her coffee cup and looked at her husband then back at me. "We thought perhaps we could have a chat before then."

"Sure. Let me see if anybody needs anything and I'll be back."

I refilled a few more cups as I wended my way to the counter, served a few more cookies, and rang up a few more tickets.

Paula came over. "Go talk to them. I can handle the people left."

I grabbed a couple of cookies for them and a glass of Coke for me. My chocolate chip cookies always put people in a better mood.

I sat down at their table. "Your son liked my cookies. I hope you do too."

"Thank you."

Warren took a bite of his. "Delicious."

Maggie nibbled at hers. A smile crinkled her eyes. "Yes, this is the kind of thing Jeff loved." She set her cookie on the plate. "Adam has always been like a son to us."

"He mentioned spending a lot of time at your house when he was young."

"Adam, Gary, and Jeff were inseparable."

"And Kathy," her husband added.

Maggie's smile disappeared. "And Kathy. She had a tough life, you know."

I sat back and crossed my arms. "I heard." Were they going to enter some kind of plea that I be kind to Kathleen? Let her have Adam because she had a tough life?

"After her dad left, her mother…" Maggie's gaze darted toward her husband as if she expected him to supply the appropriate word.

"I heard." I saved them from trying to find the word.

"She was a pretty little girl."

"Hmmm." I hadn't heard that—probably because Trent was afraid I'd hit him if he said it.

"We did everything possible to help her." Warren squeezed his wife's hand.

"She was like a sister to the boys. They shared their toys and candy with her, took care of her." Maggie folded her hands so tightly the knuckles turned white. "When kids are little, they tell outrageous stories about tigers in the back yard and invisible friends. But as they get older, they learn the difference between truth and stories."

"We teach them the difference," Warren said. "We teach our children that it's okay to tell a story for fun, but lying is wrong."

I nodded and waited. I had a feeling I knew where this was going.

"Kathy never learned the difference," Maggie said. "As she got older, she learned to be sneakier, to tell lies that sounded believable. She quit telling stories about her father coming home and bringing a suitcase full of money or her mother being an actress. Those were sad lies. But the others…" She shook her head.

"I've seen her break a toy then accuse one of the boys of doing it," Warren said.

"Whoever she accused would just drop his head and not deny it."

"And a pathological liar was born," I said.

Maggie shook her head again. "No. Pathological liars lie for no reason. Kathy always had a reason for her lies, a reason that benefited her. She lied to my son, told him Adam was abusive, that he had to save her."

Trent had said she wasn't a pathological liar. I'd thought he was defending her. Maybe he wasn't. "She's been recycling that lie about abuse. She told her current lover that your son has been beating her."

Maggie's lips compressed. "Adam asked us if that was true. My son would never hurt anyone, not even her. He was getting rid of her the right way. He was divorcing her."

"I heard."

"He told you?"

Close. Fred had told me. "He said she liked him better when he was drinking and not paying attention to her."

Maggie nodded. "After he moved to St. Louis to set up the new office, he used to come back often, sometimes for business and sometimes to visit. He always stayed with us in his old room. We could tell he wasn't happy with Kathy, but he wouldn't talk about it. He and Adam weren't friends anymore, so he spent a lot of time with Gary."

"Gary had grown up in our back yard too, so we didn't worry," Warren said. "He and Jeff did the usual guy things, like going to ball games, fishing, deer hunting. But Gary drank too much, and soon Jeff was doing the same thing."

"We can't blame Gary for that," Maggie said. "I blame Kathy."

I liked Maggie.

"He quit about a year ago," Warren said. "When he sobered up, he figured out Kathy had been spending a lot of money when he wasn't paying attention."

"A *lot* of money," Maggie repeated. "At first he was upset, but then a couple of weeks ago he said it didn't matter. He suspected she was cheating on him, and he said that didn't matter either. He said all that mattered was that he couldn't continue his life until he'd righted a terrible wrong."

"We think the wrong he needed to right was cheating on his best friend with Kathy. He said he was going to talk to Adam."

"He called him," I said. "The afternoon he was— um, Monday afternoon."

Maggie's hand lifted to her throat. "Adam didn't tell us they talked."

"They didn't. Trent didn't call him back." The words were barely out of my mouth when I wanted to recall them. I felt as if I'd betrayed Trent by admitting to Ransom's grieving parents that he'd rejected their son's attempt to make peace. "He was busy," I added. Trent was always busy, so that was the truth.

"Jeff didn't tell us he was coming to town this last time," Maggie said. "He stayed in a hotel and didn't call us. He had a reason for coming to town, something he didn't want us involved in. We believe that reason had something to do with Kathy. She followed him here."

"And she killed him," Warren said quietly.

Was the entire room suddenly silent or was our table cloaked in a special cylinder of stillness?

I took a long drink of my Coke. "Did you tell Trent your suspicions?"

"Of course we did," Warren said.

"What did he say to that?" I knew the answer already.

Maggie spread her hands, palms-up. "Nothing. He just nodded and kept asking questions."

"It's what he does," I said. "It's a cop thing." That was true, but an ugly little voice inside my head suggested Trent didn't want to think that Kathleen killed somebody, that he still harbored feelings for her. I needed to give that ugly little voice some chocolate and shut it up.

"Adam's doing the same thing he did when he was little. He's looking the other way and letting her get away with lying," Maggie said.

Warren frowned. "Letting her get away with murder."

Told you so, told you so, told you so.

Maggie leaned forward. "Will you talk to him? Will you convince him to consider her as a suspect?"

"I tried. He keeps taking up for her, making excuses for her."

That's because he still—

I coughed in an effort to drown out the sound of that obnoxious voice. *Shut up!*

Warren sighed. "After what she did to him, you'd think he'd want to prove her guilty."

"That probably makes him bend over backward not to judge her, to be fair." I dared that annoying voice to contradict me and say he still had feelings for her. *You keep mouthing off,* I warned it, *and I'll make you drink Pepsi. Diet Pepsi.*

That shut it up.

"Yes, that's probably the way Adam sees this situation. He's always given Kathy the benefit of the doubt no matter what she did. I just never thought…" Maggie's voice trailed off, not finishing the thought. *Never thought she'd kill him.*

Warren reached across the table and patted his wife's hand. She blinked back tears.

"I'm working to find evidence against her," I blurted.

They both looked at me.

"You are? Are you an investigator or something?" Maggie's gaze traveled around the room and back. "I thought you…this place…"

"Yeah, I make chocolate. I'm not an investigator. But I have a friend who…" I hesitated. I couldn't tell an outright lie, especially after hearing her disdain for Kathleen's lying. "My friend does things like tracking down killers." That was true. "He assists law enforcement sometimes." They didn't ask for his help or for mine, but we gave it to them anyway.

"Is he some kind of a special agent?" Maggie asked.

I thought about that one. "Very special."

"Can we talk to him?" Warren asked.

"I'll contact him and see if I can set up something."

Maggie squeezed my hand. "Thank you."

Warren scrawled a phone number on a napkin. "Just let us know when."

I accepted the napkin. "Your son left a key under his plate. A small key. Do you have any idea what it might go to?"

Both shook their heads.

"Jeff had one of those key rings with so many keys, it made his pocket sag," Maggie said. "He had keys to his house, our house, his offices in both cities...I have no idea what all the keys went to. Do you think it's important?"

"Maybe." Oh, good grief! I was starting to sound like Trent. "Did he ever mention hiding something from Kathleen?"

"Jeff was a very open person," Maggie said. "He's never hidden things. When he was little and it was his turn to hide the Easter eggs, he always left them in plain sight."

Had the key slipped from his wallet accidentally after all?

Even if that was true, he'd had the key in his wallet, not on his key ring. It guarded something important. The intruder in black thought so.

"If you think of anything he wanted to hide, let me know."

They nodded.

"Did your son know Trent and I were dating?"

"Oh, yes. He went online to find out how Adam was doing. A couple of months ago he said Adam was dating a wonderful girl who operated a restaurant in the space where Percy's Bar and Grill used to be."

"He knew who I was when he came in here."

"Of course."

He left the key for me, girlfriend of the cop he knew was one hundred ten percent honest.

That key was important.

The Gablers left after promising to let me know if they remembered anything else or if they came across anything with a new lock on it. In turn, I promised them I would set up an appointment with my "special agent" friend.

They were the last customers in the place so I locked the door behind them.

Paula and I divided the leftover desserts and began cleanup. While I lifted chairs onto table tops and she mopped behind me, I told her what I'd learned from the Gablers.

"That proves it," I summarized. "Kathleen murdered her husband. Trent refuses to see it because he's still taking care of her."

Paula paused and leaned on her mop. "You don't have any proof. All you have are theories. And I find it hard to believe Trent would fail to do his duty no matter what. Much as he cares for you, if you committed a crime, he'd come after you. Besides, you said Lawson's taken the lead. He has no stake in Kathleen's guilt or innocence. You and the Gablers hate her so you want her to be guilty."

I grabbed a chair, turned it over, and set it on the table. Okay, I slammed it on the table. Harder than I intended. Wood on wood. Noisy. I tried to think of a sarcastic remark to refute what she said, something that would tell her exactly what I thought of her disloyalty.

It was hard to come up with an appropriate response when she could be right.

We worked in silence, finishing the outer area and moving to the kitchen.

I closed the dishwasher door on the last load of dishes, and Paula pulled her car keys from her purse. We were ready to leave.

Someone pounded on the back door and shouted my name.

I recognized that shout.

"Go away, Rick!" I shouted back.

"You blabbed to Robin!"

Oops.

"Go away," I repeated. Neither an admission nor a denial.

"My secretary called to warn me that she's sitting in my office right now, waiting to attack me, and I have an appointment with a very important client!"

"And I don't care."

"It's your fault I can't have a business meeting in my office, so you need to let me use your place for my meeting."

I laughed. "No."

"If you don't let me in, I'll tell the cops you knew all about the drugs in that chocolate and agreed to let us deliver it here."

"Go ahead." I knew I shouldn't engage him in conversation, but I was curious about how the sting thing had gone down. This was my only chance. The cops would never tell me. They're totally into that secrecy thing. "You're still alive so I guess that means the drug deal went okay. Is Clayton alive too?"

"Of course he is." He lowered his voice and I leaned closer to the door. "The deal was a snap. That cop thing your boyfriend does, it's not so special. You should have seen me today. I had those big bad drug dealers eating out of my hand. There were two of them, and they came on all angry and threatening. One said they'd put guards on the restaurant and your house so you couldn't take their bag away, and the one on your house didn't come back. You should have heard that jerk Morton freak out. I had this thing in my ear so he could talk to me, and he almost broke my ear drum. He told me to act innocent, tell the guy I didn't know anything about it."

"Hard for you to act innocent, right?"

"I didn't get to be a top salesman by backing down when somebody brings up a problem. I took the offensive. I got right up in that guy's face and stabbed my finger into his chest. 'You put a guard on my ex-wife's house? Why did you do that? She doesn't know anything about all this. I ought to punch you.' Then I stepped back. 'So you put a guard

155

on her house and now you've lost him. What are you accusing her of? I haven't even seen your guard, but I can promise you, he's not her type.' I threw the package on the ground in front of the guy and turned around to leave. Of course he called me back. Oldest trick in the book, and he fell for it."

I leaned against the door, speechless. Drug dealers, dangerous men, and Rick saw it all as a deal. I was impressed and aghast.

"I think somebody's knocking on the front door," Paula whispered.

The front door's glass, so the sound wasn't loud. Nevertheless, I could hear it. My interior walls are thin.

"I'll go check." Paula went out front.

Rick's cell phone rang. "Hi.–Yeah, I'm almost there.–Just hang tight.–Bye." A moment of silence. "Lindsay, babe, my client's here. This is your fault. You need to make it right. Open the door."

Paula came back to the kitchen. "It's Kathleen!"

"Kathleen?" I repeated. "Your client is Kathleen?"

"She's moving back here. Going to open her own beauty supply company. I'm helping her find a place. I know you don't like her, but this is business. We'd be meeting in my office if you hadn't messed up that plan."

Kathleen had come to me. I could eavesdrop and hear what she told Rick. Of course he'd brag about outsmarting the drug dealers, and maybe she'd brag about having her husband killed.

I yanked open the door and tried to look apologetic rather than triumphant. "Rick, I'm so sorry I ruined your plans. Of course you can have your business meeting here. Come on in. Paula's going to let Kathleen in the front door."

"I am?" Paula asked.

"Of course you are."

Rick smiled and walked inside.

Sucker.

Chapter Thirteen

I led Rick into the main area of the restaurant.

Kathleen stood just inside the front door looking gorgeous, haughty, and distrustful. Her gaze settled on me. "I didn't know *she* was going to be here."

I bared my teeth in a combination smile and threat. "*She* owns this place. Have a seat at the counter—" I swept my arm toward the designated area— "and I'll bring you Cokes and cookies. We already poured out the leftover coffee, but I could make some fresh." It wouldn't be drinkable, but I didn't care.

Both of them looked at me with suspicion. Neither moved.

Maybe I was overdoing the hospitality routine.

I forced the corners of my mouth down and tried to look less like I was gloating. "I know you don't want to be here, and I don't want you here. But it's my fault you have to be. The least I can do is make you comfortable."

Paula came up behind me. "What are you doing?" she whispered.

"Paula has to leave to pick up her son, but I have things I can do in the back room to get ready for tomorrow. Feel free to take as long as you need for your meeting. You'll have complete privacy. This place was once a tavern owned by the Mafia." Rick's eyes widened. He'd brokered the deal on the place. "Before the people we bought it from," I added. "And right behind those swinging doors to the kitchen is a soundproof, bulletproof pocket door."

Yes, it was a lie. Not about the pocket door. It existed as a way to completely close off the rooms. We'd never used the door. It was flimsy and far from soundproof or bulletproof. However, lying to Rick or Kathleen didn't count as a real lie since they did it so often. A reciprocal lie balanced out the universe.

Rick was the first to cave. He squeezed my arm briefly. "Thank you for being so gracious about this." He moved to the counter and motioned Kathleen to join him.

She crossed the room, her gaze never leaving mine. I sent all my brain power to her stiletto heels, willing one of them to trip on the smooth tile. It didn't happen. I should have eaten more chocolate to increase my brain power.

She eased onto a stool beside Rick.

"Okay," I said, "I'll get those cookies and be out of your way."

I took Paula's arm and urged her toward the kitchen.

For somebody so small, she's quite difficult to *urge.*

As soon as we were in the kitchen she dragged me over to the far corner of the room. "What are you thinking, letting those people use this place for a meeting?" she whispered.

I lifted a finger to my lips. I didn't want *those people* to realize how easy it was to hear from the other room. "Go pick up Zack. I've got this."

"No way am I leaving you alone with those two."

"Hah. You should be worried about leaving those two alone with me. Look, I'm just going to listen to what they have to say, then we'll all leave."

"As soon as I get Zach, I'm coming back."

A burst of laughter exploded from the front area.

"Really? You want to expose your three year old son to *those people?*"

Paula drew in a deep breath and closed her eyes for a moment as if trying to shut out the circumstances around her. "I didn't lock the front door because I thought she'd be going right back out through it."

"No problem. I'll take care of it. I don't want them to escape."

"Be careful. Those two are nothing but trouble."

I lifted her purse and her bag of leftover goodies from the counter. "Go! Zach's waiting. The babysitter may kick him out and he'll wander the streets looking for you until he's an old man because you didn't have him chipped like I did Henry."

She left reluctantly.

I grabbed my bag of desserts and headed back to *those two*.

They were cozy, heads close together, laughing. They looked up when I entered. Rick wore his salesman-of-the-year expression and Kathleen wore her hooker-of-the-year expression.

"All righty," I said. "I have chocolate chip cookies, brownies, and a couple pieces of Chocolate Caramel Peanut Butter Cake."

Kathleen turned up her perky little nose. Another creation of the plastic surgeon? "No, thank you."

"None for me," Rick said. "I could go for a glass of water, though."

"You bet. Sure you don't want a Coke? How about you, Kathleen?"

"Nothing for me."

I gave Rick a glass of water. "When you're ready to leave, open the swinging doors and bang on the interior door really loud because I won't be able to hear you unless you make a loud noise because it's totally soundproof."

I pushed through the swinging doors and peeked back at them. They were already cozy again, heads together, laughing.

My ex was flirting with Trent's ex. That was some serious Jerry Springer type stuff.

I slid the pocket door closed and pressed my ear to it. I could still hear them as if the door was made of paper.

Just to be sure I didn't miss anything, I grabbed a glass and climbed onto the counter between the kitchen and the outer room. Most of the wall was covered with cabinets, but an area over the sink was clear. I leaned into that space.

It was not a comfortable position, and when my cell phone started to ring, I almost fell in my effort to yank it out of my pocket and answer before the people in the other room realized that if they could hear my cell phone, I might be able to hear them.

It was Trent. Only time I haven't been happy to hear from him. "Hello."

"Why are you whispering?"

I leaned around a cabinet and faced away from the wall. "Frog in my throat." Amphibian in my throat, snakes in the other room.

"Want to go to dinner with Gary tonight at Capelli's about seven?"

"Sure. Bye." I set my phone on vibrate and returned my attention to eavesdropping.

I needn't have rushed my call with Trent. Before long I was sore and bored.

Rick told his story of the morning's events, embellishing even more than when he told me the story earlier.

Yawn.

Kathleen didn't reciprocate with her own story of misdeeds. Instead she told him what a brave man he was.

Gag.

Finally Rick brought up the subject of business.

I wasn't surprised when she rambled aimlessly about what type structure she needed. She had no business plan. Had she just set up this meeting with Rick to flirt with him?

"I'll get a little money from my husband's insurance policies," she said (a *little*?), "but not enough to live on. I need to invest in some kind of business."

"If you're interested in purchasing real estate strictly as an investment, I can help you with that. There are several different directions we could go, all of them profitable."

"That might be a good choice. I don't have a lot of job skills. My husband didn't want me to work. He was abusive and didn't want me out in the world, meeting other people, telling them what he did to me, letting them see my bruises."

"I'm so sorry." Rick's words of sympathy dripped with the insincere tones of a con man.

"It does something to a woman's soul to be hit by a man."

She was bragging again, claiming to have a soul.

"I can't imagine why a man would ever hit a woman."

He sounded so sanctimonious, I wanted to climb off the counter, charge into the other room, and confront him.

Cheat, steal, lie, berate, and demean a woman, that was okay. Everything was fine as long as he didn't hit her.

But I was on a mission and we were headed in the right direction. Kathleen was talking about her husband.

Super salesman Rick brought the subject back to investing in real estate. Damn him and his greedy little heart.

A bell jingled.

I had forgotten to lock the front door. Was Kathleen escaping before I got anything usable from her?

I started to climb down.

"What are you doing here?" Kathleen from the other room. Obviously she hadn't escaped. Someone had entered. Someone she knew. Someone she didn't want to see, judging by the panic in her voice.

I climbed back up and pressed my glass to the wall.

"I followed you here," a man shouted loudly enough I could have heard him if I'd been standing outside in the alley. "The big question is, what are *you* doing here?"

The man's voice was familiar. If he'd speak in normal tones, I was sure I'd recognize him.

"I'm having a business meeting with this gentleman." Kathleen's voice was indignant with a hint of fear.

"Rick Kramer. I'm with Rheims Commercial Real Estate."

"I know who you are."

And suddenly I knew who the new participant was.

Corey. Ransom's protégé and Kathleen's lover.

"Mrs. Gabler and I were discussing some options for real estate investments," Rick said.

"Oh yeah? Well, I've been watching you, and I'd say the only thing going on here is you seducing my fiancé."

His *fiancé*?

"I can assure you, no such thing is happening. Kathleen…Mrs. Gabler…maybe we'd better reschedule."

That's my Rick. Run at the first sign of trouble.

"I'll call you," Kathleen said.

The bell jingled again. Either another player had come in or one had left. I assumed Rick had left the building.

"I thought you were going back to St. Louis," Kathleen said.

"And I thought you were going to get your hair done," Corey accused.

"I have an appointment in an hour."

"You didn't say anything about meeting with some sleazy real estate salesman."

Corey was amazingly perceptive about Rick.

"I don't have to tell you everything I do. I can't believe you followed me!"

"I can't believe I have to follow you to find out what you're doing. I knew something was going on. You've been avoiding me."

"We agreed we shouldn't be seen together for a while. I took a big chance, spending the night with you."

"I'm tired of hiding. We've been doing that for almost a year. Jeff's dead. We can be together in public now."

"You don't think that might seem a little suspicious?" She lowered her voice so I could barely hear. "My husband's been murdered, I'm the beneficiary of his life insurance, and you're my lover. You don't think that's going to put us both on the suspect list? That detective, Lawson, has been harassing me, asking me all kinds of questions about my relationship with Jeff."

"Don't answer any questions without your lawyer."

"I know that, but the man is really annoying. He's not as easy to put off as Adam."

Not as easy to put off as Adam? She was going to pay for that remark. Or Trent was. Depending on whether it was the truth or a brag.

"He came by to see me too. I told him about Jeff's drinking problem and the spousal abuse. We're fine. You need to stop worrying."

"And you need to leave, now. Get back to St. Louis and let me take care of things here."

"Things like that salesman? I saw your text messages to him. I know you told him you're moving back here. Where does that leave us? I work in St. Louis. You're supposed to be marrying me!"

"You looked at my phone? You had no right to do that!"

"I killed a man for you. I think that gives me a few rights."

I nearly dropped my glass, fumbled for it, and almost fell from my precarious perch.

Had I heard right? Had Corey just confessed to murder? And he'd done it for *her*?

My theory was right.

I couldn't wait to tell Trent.

I pressed the glass back to the wall. I'd hoped for comments I could follow up on. I hadn't expected a confession. This was like expecting vanilla ice cream and getting a hot fudge sundae with whipped cream and chopped nuts.

"What kind of rights do you think you'll have if we both get sent to prison? Get out of here. I'll deal with Rick, though now I may have to sleep with him to make him forget he saw you. If I do, it's your fault. If you'd gone back home when I told you to, everything would be fine."

"Lindsay, come down from there."

I gasped at the soft voice behind me, fumbled and grabbed futilely at a cabinet. My hand slid across the smooth surface.

Fred clutched my shoulders and stopped my fall.

I scrambled to get back up, but he halted my progress. "There's a better way to do that, one that doesn't involve killing yourself or throwing your back out," he whispered.

"What are you doing here?"

"Paula and Zach came by to tell me you needed help. It appears they were right." He reached inside his pocket, withdrew two ear buds, handed one to me, and put the other in his own ear. Next he produced a small metal rectangle which he held against the wall.

Silence then the sound of the bell over the front door jingling.

My heart sank. One or both of them had left.

I eased back the pocket door and peered into the room.

The place was empty.

I ran to the door and looked out. "They escaped!"

"I think they'll be relatively easy to find."

I spun around to face Fred. "Corey confessed! They're murderers! They could be halfway to Mexico by now!"

"Corey confessed?"

It was worth every pain of standing over that sink to see a surprised look on Fred's face. That doesn't happen often.

"Yes, he did. He said he killed a man for *her*."

"Interesting. Why don't you lock the front door and let's have some chocolate and talk."

This was definitely one of my proudest moments. I'd surprised Fred.

I locked the front door. "Let me get my bag of goodies from the kitchen," I said. "Go ahead and pour us some Cokes."

Too cool. We were having a discussion about my findings.

When I returned with my chocolate leftovers, Fred had drinks, plates, and forks waiting. I served us each a piece of Chocolate Caramel Peanut Butter Cake.

He took a bite. "Delicious, as always."

"So now all I have to do is tell Trent, he'll arrest both of them, and everything will return to normal."

"It will give the police something to go on, but it's not a done deal. Your testimony would be hearsay."

"But I heard him say it!" I listened to my own words. *Heard...say.* Hearsay. I chugged the remainder of my Coke, trying to drown my sorrows. "I have to do something to get enough evidence to send Kathleen to prison."

"How are you going to do that?"

"I'm not sure. You have any ideas?"

"We could capture her, tie her to a chair in my basement, and use cattle prods on her until she confesses."

"You have cattle prods?"

"It was a joke."

"Damn. I was looking forward to going all Jack Bauer on her." He cleverly avoided my question as to whether he had cattle prods. If I ever needed to prod any cattle, I'd check back with him. "If we must, we'll come up with something that doesn't involve torture."

"Like what?"

"This is off the top of my head so it may need some refining. What if I tell Kathleen that Ransom left me a key and told me if anything happens to him, I should reveal the secret it guards at his memorial service? That gives her a short deadline."

Fred frowned. "And then?"

"She comes after me to get the key, and that proves her guilt."

"Actually, it wouldn't prove anything except that she wanted the key. What if she sends Corey after you to get the key and dispose of you because you know too much?"

I slid off my stool and gathered up our dishes. "I'm not worried. You'll be right around the corner with one of your gadgets recording the entire conversation. You've never let me get killed yet."

"I don't like that idea. Let's go back to the cattle prods."

"Okay." I liked my idea and I wasn't about to give up.

He narrowed his eyes. "I know what *okay* means. Don't do it. Don't put yourself in danger. We'll find another way."

"Okay." I tried to look innocent. "Anyway, how do you think I'd get her to meet with me in the first place? It's not like we're best buds and I can just text her and ask her to do lunch."

He rose from his stool and looked at me for several seconds, his lips slowly curving upward. "Let me know when you get that meeting scheduled."

I smiled. He was in. "I need her cell phone number."

"If I give you her number, you have to promise to let me know every detail of what you're doing, what she says, where and when you're meeting her."

"Of course. Don't I always?"

He said nothing.

"Well, this afternoon was spontaneous. Not planned."

He still said nothing.

"It's not like I was in any danger!"

He continued to say nothing very loudly.

"All right, all right! I promise!"

"I'll text you her number when we get home."

"What can I say to her to make sure she comes?"

He said some more of that *nothing*, turned and headed toward the kitchen and the exit.

Never hurts to ask.

Sometimes it doesn't help either.

Chapter Fourteen

As I drove home, I formulated a plan. Tonight I would be with two of the men in Kathleen's life…Trent and Gary. I should be able to lure her to Capelli's where I could taunt her about the key in complete safety, maybe even freak her out enough she'd confess in front of Trent.

When I got home and opened my front door, Henry glared at me and stalked toward the kitchen. I was late. He was upset. A little food, a few mice, and he'd be happy again. He may be a cat, but he's still a guy.

While he ate, I dashed upstairs and showered then dressed in my best jeans, the ones with rhinestones and metal studs. Since purple is a royal color, I chose a purple blouse. Yes, a real blouse, not a T-shirt. I even put on makeup. With my coloring, there's a fine line between looking like a ghost or a clown. I did my best to straddle that line.

When I checked my cell phone, I found Fred's text with Kathleen's number.

I sat on the bed and started a message to that number. I got as far as *Kathleen* then stared at the phone.

Fred could have come up with something creative, something that would make her drop everything and dash down to the restaurant. I'm creative with chocolate but that's about it.

I rubbed my nose. I read somewhere that increases the flow of blood to the brain.

It did not increase the flow of ideas for getting Kathleen to Capelli's.

I tried to think like Fred but that made my brain feel twisted and weird.

I finally gave up and decided to think like Lindsay.

Capelli's at 7:30. Come alone.

If I got a message like that, I'd have to follow up. I could only hope she was the curious type.

I kept my word and texted Fred to tell him what I'd done.

I needed a prop, something I could pretend held the key Ransom gave me.

A tin of mints rested on my nightstand between my lamp and my iron skillet. Perfect.

I dumped the mints onto a tissue.

The box would work.

It would work even better if I put a real key in it to rattle around.

I had lots of unidentified keys. I opened my nightstand drawer, rummaged through the contents, and came up with one. It was small and not too different than the real key Ransom had left for me. Not that I intended to show Kathleen, but it should make the appropriate rattling sound.

I transferred the contents of my regular black leather purse into my fancy black leather purse with metal studs. I felt empowered with all the bling. I tossed in my cell phone and put the tin in a side pocket for easy access.

Thus prepared, I went downstairs to let Henry out for his evening of fun and frivolity.

As I stood on the porch watching him stroll leisurely into the night, Trent pulled into the driveway and parked behind my car.

"Hey, good-looking," I called. "Come inside and I'll show you a good time." Though telling him I'd heard his ex-wife's boyfriend confess to murdering on her behalf might not be his idea of a good time.

"Hey, beautiful, I'm up for that." He came over and gave me a quick kiss. "You look great. How was your day?"

"Long and eventful."

He held the door for me. "Tell me."

"Let's sit down with a Coke. Maybe two."

We went inside and I fetched a couple of Cokes then sat beside him on the sofa.

I popped the top on my can and decided to start with the first event. Sort of like the warm-up band at a concert. "You'll never guess who came to visit me today. Maggie and Warren Gabler."

"Oh?"

Maybe I shouldn't have told him. They had, after all, come to me because they didn't think Trent believed Kathleen killed their son.

"Nice people." I took a drink to give me time to decide how much of the conversation I should tell him. Not telling him everything wasn't the same as lying. Yeah, I've heard that *lying by omission* theory, but I don't subscribe to it. Who tells everything they know? How boring would that be? *I got up this morning and I took a shower and I put on my clothes and I fed Henry and I got in my car…*

ZZZZZZZZZZZZ…

"Yes, they are. What did you talk about?"

I shrugged. "You, Gary, their son, Kathleen. I gave them some of my chocolate chip cookies and they liked them." I didn't feel comfortable admitting that the Gablers wanted me to convince him Kathleen had murdered their son, and I didn't have to. All I had to do was tell him about Corey's confession and her response.

I set my can on the coffee table and perched on the edge of the sofa with my hands wrapped around my knees. "But the real news happened later after Rick and Kathleen came to my restaurant." I got his attention with that statement. "While they were there, Corey Paggett burst in and accused her of cheating on him. Rick left, and Corey said he committed murder for her."

I might have been telling him about getting up in the morning, taking a shower, getting dressed, and feeding Henry for all the emotion Trent revealed.

"Go on." No emotion in his voice either.

He was doing that cop thing again.

I licked my lips. "Then she…" I hesitated. Kathleen hadn't actually admitted to being a part of the murder. "Then she said, um, that she'd deal with Rick and she might have to sleep with him to make him forget he saw Corey and that Corey should have gone back to St. Louis."

Trent waited.

My tongue had suddenly grown to fill my entire mouth. "And that's all," I mumbled.

He waited.

Of all the possible reactions I'd considered he might have...shock, sadness, horror, happiness, denial...I hadn't expected no reaction.

"I know it's hearsay, but we can use it to get a confession. Right?"

He took my hand. "I promise you, the police department is investigating this crime. We've got everything under control."

I had come to him with serious evidence, and he was brushing me off, assuring the little lady that the big cops were taking care of it and didn't need her help.

I bit back a snarky retort.

I also bit back the urge to tell him of my clever plan to get Kathleen to join us for dinner. He might not think it was all that clever considering his reaction to my news. He might be a little irritated with me.

There was no point in telling him about it when she might not even show up.

If she did, I'd deal with it then.

Tonight could be very interesting.

Or a total disaster.

If she didn't show up, I couldn't give her my message about the key.

If she did show up, Trent would probably not be happy.

I wasn't sure which scenario I was hoping for.

"Ready to go?" he asked.

"Sure. Let me grab a jacket." I opened the coat closet and took out my favorite denim jacket, the one with rhinestones and metal studs. More bling. More empowerment. I was ready to face Kathleen.

We drove to the small restaurant in downtown Pleasant Grove. Since it was only a few blocks from the Pleasant Grove Manor, Kathleen shouldn't have any trouble getting there, should she feel so inclined.

Trent pulled into the parking lot behind the restaurant. The building was about the same age as the hotel and had originally been a bank. The words *First National Bank of Pleasant Grove* were still engraved in the marble over the ornate door.

Legend has it that a member of the Kansas City mafia converted the bank to a family-owned restaurant back in the fifties, and the wife of the current owner is a direct descendant of the mafia owner. Fred told me the woman's birth name was Jones, so I doubt the mafia story is true. But it lends a certain ambiance to the place.

We walked from the chill of the evening into warmth and delicious smells. Soft lighting muted the red and white checks of the tablecloths and the red vinyl of the booths. The place was crowded, but the conversations were murmurs thanks to the addition of modern acoustical tiles.

Gary was already there. He and Trent did the man half-hug thing. Then he turned to me and wrapped me in a real embrace. He didn't hold too tightly or press himself against me or anything gross. He smelled of some kind of woodsy cologne that reminded me more of one of those green trees hanging from a rear view mirror than the great outdoors though it wasn't horrible. There was no reason for me to feel repulsed, but I did.

I'd seen him open the door to let Kathleen inside. That image was stuck in my brain. I put one arm around him and patted him on the back then pulled away.

The hostess led us to a booth halfway across the room. What if Kathleen didn't see us?

Gary started to sit on the side facing the door.

"Wait!" I said. "We need to sit on that side."

"We do?" Trent asked.

"Ever since the incident with that guy, I just can't stand to sit with my back to the door." There'd been more than one incident with more than one guy, so that should work.

Trent nodded. "I understand."

Gary moved to the other side.

Trent politely waited for me to sit first.

"I need to be on the outside. I've been drinking a lot of Coke."

After much effort, I finally ended up on the outside seat, facing the door.

Gary ordered a bottle of Chianti then made a big deal of sniffing the cork, swirling the sample poured by the waitress, sniffing again, and sipping before he proclaimed it, "Good."

He did have a rather large nose. Perhaps made his sense of smell more acute.

Yes, I was being snide. I didn't like him simply because Kathleen had gone to his house. Any friend of hers was an enemy of mine.

Trent allowed the waitress to pour wine for him. That surprised me. He's such a stickler for following the rules. *If you drink, don't drive.*

As soon as the waitress left, Gary lifted his glass. "To Jeff, our friend. We had some good times. He will be missed."

Trent joined in the toast but took only a small sip of wine. So did I. He was watching his alcohol intake so he could drive safely. I was watching mine so I could be coherent enough to take on Kathleen.

Gary took another drink. "Remember when we almost burned down Jeff's house?"

Trent shifted slightly and grimaced. "I'd just as soon forget about that."

"No, man, it's a great story." Gary turned to me. "We were playing in the snow in Jeff's back yard. It was really cold, but we didn't want to go inside. We were all in the Boy Scouts, and that summer we camped out and learned how to build fires. We decided instead of giving up our play time and going in, we'd make a fire to warm up."

"A fire?" I asked. "In the snow?"

"They had three big pine trees, and the ground under them was sheltered from the snow. We thought that would be a good place to start."

Trent focused his attention on twirling his wine glass, but a faint smile tilted his lips. "We were kids. Dumb kids. Gary took out his pocket knife and shaved some sticks into kindling. Do you remember that knife? It had a blade for everything. You loved that knife."

Gary nodded. "My old man gave it to me. It came in handy for a lot of things, but it wasn't much help that day."

"Dumb kids," Trent said again. "Not only was our kindling wet, we couldn't get anything to spark. We twirled sticks and hit rocks together."

Gary grinned. "But then Kathleen showed up with her mother's cigarette lighter. Adam said that was cheating, but we got our fire started."

Some things don't change. Trent played by the rules and Kathleen caused problems.

Trent swirled the wine in his glass. "And the tree."

"The tree?" I repeated.

Gary flinched and had another drink of wine. "Yeah, our fire got a little out of control. Some of the branches were drooping pretty low, and it seems pine needles burn very easily."

Trent set his glass on the table. "Fortunately, the snow on the tree put out the fire but not before Jeff's dad saw it and came rushing out of the house with a fire extinguisher. He was upset with all of us. And then I had to go home and hear about it all over again from my parents."

Gary finished his wine and poured more in his glass. "Your folks and Jeff's were pretty strict."

"Not really."

I waited for Trent to elaborate. Did that mean Gary's parents were lenient? I had already figured out that Kathleen's mother had no idea what she was doing and didn't care. A cigarette lighter?

The waitress arrived with our salads. Gary ordered another bottle of wine.

He and Ransom had been drinking buddies. Apparently Gary had not quit.

I was eating the last bite of my Caesar salad when Kathleen walked through the door in her stiletto heels and tight, short black dress.

Yes!

She paused and looked around the room. Searching for us or just checking to see if all the men were ogling her?

I didn't want to be obvious, but I didn't want her to miss us. I lifted the hand holding my fork and waved it around. "This is just a wonderful place. I'm so happy we came here."

Trent paused with a bite of salad halfway to his mouth. "I'm glad you like it." His voice had that *Have you been drinking too much wine?* edge to it.

The hostess approached Kathleen. The two of them spoke for a moment then Kathleen headed straight toward us.

I braced myself. I had no idea what she was going to say, and I had no idea how Trent was going to react. Most importantly, I had no idea how long she'd stay, how much time I would have to put my plan into play.

Kathleen stopped at our booth. "What a coincidence we all decided to eat here tonight."

We were off to a good start. She was going to play innocent and so was I.

Trent looked at her then at me.

He wasn't buying the innocent thing.

"I'm here all by lonesome," she said. "If nobody's sitting here, can I join you?"

"Please do." Gary patted the bench next to him. "We just finished our salads, but you can catch up."

Kathleen slid into the booth and smiled at Gary then Trent. "Thank you."

She was still smiling when her gaze landed on me, but by then it was more of a *This better be good or I'm going to kill you* expression.

Gary waved the waitress over to take Kathleen's order. She selected one of the low calorie, low fat items. Skinny bitch.

I'd ordered lasagna. I intended to eat it in front of her and enjoy every cheesy, calorie-laden bite.

The waitress brought another wine glass. Kathleen took small sips of her wine. The level in the bottle was going down mostly through Gary's efforts.

I folded my hands on the table and prepared to launch into my program. "Have you three worked out all the details of the memorial service?"

"Pretty much," Trent said.

"Most of it," Gary confirmed.

"Will you have time for friends to speak?" I asked.

Gary nodded. "Sure."

"Ransom—Jeff—gave me a key before he left my place." I reached into my bag and pulled out the small tin, rattling it for effect. "He asked me to keep it for him. Said he'd come back the next day and get it. But if he didn't come back, if anything happened to him, I was to retrieve what this key guards the morning of his memorial service and present it at the service."

I was deliberately not looking at Trent, but in my peripheral vision, I could see his expression. Aghast.

Kathleen lifted her wine glass. "What a charming story. My husband decides to leave a key that unlocks a secret treasure for a total stranger to find and bring to his funeral. Have you ever thought about a career in writing? You'd probably be better at it than you are at making chocolate desserts."

My jaw locked. I froze in place.

For trying to take my boyfriend, I was going to kill her. For insulting my chocolate, I was going to torture her with Fred's cattle prods for several hours before killing her.

Trent cleared his throat. "Lindsay's desserts are wonderful. Gary, have you tried her chocolate chip cookies?"

"No, I haven't, but it's on my list."

Maybe Gary wasn't so bad after all.

"We should meet there for lunch tomorrow," Trent said.

"I wouldn't miss it." Kathleen's smile compressed into a smirk.

Great. That woman was coming back to my place to dine with my boyfriend.

"What time?" Gary asked.

Trent looked at me. "What would be the best time?"

Two hours after closing time when I'm long gone. "Things slow down around 1:00."

Gary took out his cell phone and began tapping. He returned it to the inside pocket of his sports coat then looked around and grinned lopsidedly. "Sorry. Didn't mean to be rude. Habit. If I don't put an appointment in my calendar immediately, I'll forget it. Am I the only one who can't live without my cell phone?"

Kathleen opened her designer bag and extracted hers. "I wouldn't want to be late."

Trent shrugged and took his phone from his jacket pocket. "I think I can probably remember, but why take a chance?"

"I'm pretty sure I'll be there without a reminder." I lifted my glass for another drink of wine. Maybe Gary had the right idea.

The waitress arrived with our food.

Gary ordered another bottle.

That was probably a good decision. My glass was mysteriously empty.

I made a show of putting the tin back in my purse, took a bite of lasagna and considered how I could salvage the evening. Leaping across the table and plunging my fork into her heart was not a viable option. The tines weren't long enough or sharp enough to pierce those implants.

"Ransom was in fear for his life when he came to me," I said. "He didn't know who to trust. We bonded. He loved my chocolate chip cookies."

"Why do you keep calling him that strange name?" Kathleen asked.

"That's what he said he liked to be called. You don't know a lot about your past husbands, do you?"

Kathleen held a bite of chicken poised a few inches from her mouth. "More than you do." Her lips tilted into a mean smile. She parted them, moved the chicken inside, and chewed slowly, her gaze never leaving mine.

I might be able to slit her throat with the bread knife.

"Why didn't you use the key and bring this mysterious object tonight?" she asked.

This lying business was more complicated than I'd thought. I had another bite of lasagna to give me time to think. "My instructions are to retrieve it an hour before the service. Ransom said I'd understand everything when I saw it and that a lot of people would be very surprised."

"Why wait? It's not like Jeff's going to find out you disobeyed his instructions and get mad at you."

"He might. Are you saying you don't believe the spirits of departed people can contact us?"

Kathleen leaned close to Gary and whispered something in his ear.

They both laughed.

I seethed.

"Gary, you think the Chiefs have a chance to make Super Bowl this year?" Trent asked.

Kathleen dissed my chocolate and my boyfriend wanted to talk about football.

The evening could not possibly get any worse.

By the time we walked out of the restaurant into the chilly night, Gary was staggering noticeably. He wrapped an arm around Kathleen. The gesture appeared to be more for the purpose of staying upright than affection. She was half his size and wearing those ridiculous heels. No good could come of this. She made a futile attempt to extricate herself.

Trent halted. "Gary—"

He looked at Trent then wavered briefly with one foot on the curb and the other in mid-air. The result was inevitable. Gary and Kathleen tumbled to the street together.

Gary grunted.

Kathleen screamed.

Trent swore. He leaned over the fallen couple, reaching for Kathleen's shoulder.

Gary grabbed Trent's arm and tried to stand. Well, I think that's what he was attempting. What he accomplished was to pull Trent into the fray.

Kathleen screamed again, kicked and pummeled Gary, and called him some very unflattering names. I was amazed the woman had a good vocabulary of anything, even swear words.

Trent finally extricated himself, shoved Gary away and pulled Kathleen to her feet. "Are you okay?"

She stumbled. "I think my ankle's broken!"

Served her right for wearing those stupid heels.

Gary struggled to his feet. "I'm sorry, Kathy. I'm so sorry." He ran a hand through his hair. "I think I had too much to drink."

"You think?" Kathleen stood on one foot, using Trent to steady herself. Woman had terrible balance. She shouldn't have had to wrap both arms around him.

Too bad it was her ankle that was broken. If anyone had asked for my input, I'd have voted for her neck.

Nobody asked me.

They never do.

"I'll drive you back to your hotel room, Kathy, then take Gary home. I don't think you ought to be driving tonight, buddy. We'll come back tomorrow for your car."

Gary straightened. "I'm okay." He swayed from side to side though there was no wind. "I'll take Kathy home."

"You've done enough for one night." Kathleen put her injured foot on the ground, winced, and lifted it again. "Adam's taking me to the emergency room, and you can sleep it off in the gutter."

Gary's arms fell limply to his sides. "Don't be that way, Kathy."

Yeah, don't be that way. Don't volunteer my boyfriend to take you to the hospital.

Trent looked at me, his expression somewhere between apologetic and accusatory. "Lindsay has to get up early in the morning. I'll take her home first, drop you off at your house, Gary, and take Kathy to the emergency room."

I was wrong. Things could and did get worse. I'd set out to prove Kathleen's guilt and convince Trent she was a murderer. I'd succeeded in upsetting him, being insulted by Kathleen, and would end the evening in my bed alone while Trent waited at the emergency room with Kathleen.

Good job, Lindsay.

Chapter Fifteen

The drive to my house was short in miles but long in duration. Trent stared straight ahead into the darkness of the night and spoke not a word. I did the same.

In the back seat Kathleen gave an occasional whimper when we hit a bump. Gary snored.

I got out as soon as the car rolled to a stop in front of my house.

"Wait," Trent said. "Let me walk you to your door."

I didn't want him to do that. He was probably going to get on my case about inviting Kathleen to dinner or taunting her with the key or the entire dinner debacle. Justifiably, perhaps, but I still didn't want to hear it, didn't want him to be angry with me.

"I know the way."

He strode around the car toward me. "So do the local drug dealers."

Would I rather face the dangerous drug dealers or my angry boyfriend?

Henry trotted out of the night, across Fred's yard to mine.

I live under the protective auspices of a vicious feline and a neighbor who has super powers.

I'd rather face the dangerous drug dealers.

Trent caught up to me and took my hand.

Neither Henry nor Fred could help me now.

We walked to the front door. Trent used the key I'd given him. "Wait here while I check things out."

He and Henry went inside. I could have told Trent no evil waited within. Henry would not be calm if an unknown person lurked. But I let him do his cop thing while I stood on the porch shivering.

He returned shortly. "Looks okay. I'll get back here as quick as I can. In the meantime, put chairs under the door knobs of your front and back doors. Don't let anyone in but me. If you hear or see anyone else, call Fred, me, and 911, in that order."

I don't like anybody telling me what to do, but it was sweet that he cared. Really sweet that he was only concerned about my safety and not the events at dinner.

We shared a kiss, a sweet, sexy kiss.

He placed a hand on my chin and gazed into my eyes. "When I get back, we'll talk about what happened at dinner."

Of course he wasn't going to let me off so easily.

He left, not exactly on a romantic note.

I closed the door behind him then brought in a chair to put under the door knob and went to the kitchen to do likewise for the back door.

Henry watched my actions with a bored gaze. As soon as I secured the chair in the kitchen, he darted to the drawer where I kept the catnip.

I thought about it. If I had a return visit from the guy in the mask, I needed Henry awake and alert. But

Trent would be back soon. He'd be able to take care of the masked man.

I would have to be awake to move the chair and let him in so he could yell at me. Henry didn't need to hear any of that.

I gave him some catnip in a saucer, sat down at the kitchen table to watch him devour it, and called Fred.

"I've been waiting to hear from you," he said. "How did the evening go?"

"Not well." I gave him the details.

"If Kathleen has a broken ankle, she probably won't be coming after you to get that key."

"I don't think it's broken. I think she just used that as a way to get Trent all to herself."

"That's possible."

I set my elbow on the table, put my head on my hand, and sighed.

Henry looked up at the sound then returned to inhaling his kitty weed.

"This wasn't one of my better ideas. I didn't learn anything new, and Kathleen insulted me and walked away with my guy. The only good thing about the evening was the food."

"Maybe not. You may have stirred up more than you realize. If Kathleen's involved, she's managed to get you home alone with no protection."

I looked at Henry. He purred loudly and rolled his face in the empty saucer.

No protection? How did he know Henry was stoned? "I have an iron skillet and a marble rolling pin and you next door."

"Someone may decide to take the opportunity to retrieve that key before you have a chance to unlock the mystery."

"That was the plan, but I don't think it's going to happen."

"If you see or hear anything suspicious, call me no matter what time it is."

"I'll keep my skillet and rolling pin close."

"And your cell phone."

I sighed again. "Yeah, yeah, yeah. I already got that same order from Trent. I'm not helpless, you know."

"I didn't say you were. However, I've provided information and assistance in this matter. I don't want to be left out of the final chapter."

"That makes sense. I'll call you immediately if I have the slightest hint something's coming down."

He hung up.

I looked at Henry. "Yes, I know Fred only said that to save my pride, and it worked. Just don't tell anybody, okay?"

Henry returned my gaze, his big blue eyes slightly crossed.

I shook my head. "What am I saying? You're stoned. You won't remember a thing about this tomorrow." I rose from the table. "I'm going to make some hot chocolate and read a book while we wait for Trent."

Pointless talking to a stoned cat.

I made my hot chocolate and took it into the living room. Henry joined me on the sofa. I laid my cell phone on the nearest lamp table and cradled the steaming beverage in both hands, absorbing the heat and breathing deeply of the chocolate fumes.

The first sip of the liquid ambrosia warmed me from the inside out and soothed my worries. I retrieved my book from the coffee table and settled in for a short wait. The hospital wasn't far, and once the doctor took a look at Kathleen's ankle and pronounced her a malingerer, Trent would head home to me.

My phone rang.

I lifted it and looked at the screen. I didn't recognize the number. Surely no salesman would call at almost ten o'clock at night.

I answered.

"Lindsay, it's Maggie Gabler. I apologize for calling so late."

"No problem. I'm up."

"Is Adam with you?"

"He will be shortly."

"You asked us about a key Jeff left for you."

I sat upright so rapidly my cocoa sloshed and almost spilled. "Yes?"

Henry lifted his head and regarded me through narrowed eyes.

"This is probably silly…"

"Go on."

"Jeff's toy chest in his room. It has a padlock on it. A new padlock."

I relaxed back into the sofa. "His toy chest?"

Henry closed his eyes and lowered his head.

"It's a big wooden chest his dad made for him when he was a boy. When he was older, he stored books and games and whatever was important to him in it. It's never before had a lock on it. He must have put it on during one of his recent visits."

His toy chest. I wasn't sure if I should be elated or deflated.

"Is it a big padlock?"

"No, just the regular size."

"Maybe you could snip it and see what's inside."

"Yes, we could. Warren and I talked about that, but it would be invading Jeff's privacy. If there's something in there he doesn't want us to see, we don't intend to look. We thought maybe you and Adam could come over tomorrow and bring the key. If it opens the padlock, that means he wanted you to see what's inside."

"Sure. We can do that." I had no idea how long the meeting with Trent, Gary, and Kathleen would last. Surely not more than an hour or two. "How about around 4:30 or 5:00? I'll talk to Trent and get back to you with a more definite time."

"That sounds great."

We hung up and I sat staring at the phone but not really seeing it.

His toy chest.

Was the key unimportant after all?

Or had he stored something important in his toy chest?

If so, was it something important to solving his murder or was it some boyhood treasure he wanted Trent to have?

My cell phone tinkled like a wind chime. Text message.

I looked at the screen.

Text message from Trent.

Please come to the hospital. I need you.

I smiled. He needed me.

What's wrong? I texted back.

Long story. I'll tell you when I see you. I'm in the emergency waiting room.

I was glad I hadn't changed into my sexy purple flannel pajamas yet.

I took one more sip of my hot chocolate, retrieved my jacket from the closet, and headed out the door.

I felt a little guilty about leaving Henry alone in the house in his inebriated state, but even if someone broke in, they'd just tear the house apart looking for that key. They'd have no reason to harm a stoned cat.

My purse played the theme song from Game of Thrones. I hesitated but only for an instant. It was my generic ring tone...not Trent, not Fred, not Paula. Maybe the Gablers calling again. I'd call them back when I got to the hospital. Trent needed me.

As I dashed across the yard through the chilly darkness to my beloved elderly car, I had a fleeting disloyal wish that it was newer, that I could start it remotely and warm it up. I park it in the driveway since a strong wind could blow over my garage...and Kansas City has a lot of strong winds. The doors no longer seal as tightly as they once did, and I knew it would already be cold.

I opened the door, slid in, and patted the dashboard. "I don't really wish you were newer."

The engine cranked immediately. So it has a few dents, the radio doesn't work, the doors don't seal, and a few other inconsequential things are wrong. The important parts still function great.

I put the car into reverse.

The scent of a pine tree deodorizer drifted through the car.

Couldn't be. I never used those things.

I backed down the driveway into the street.

Pine tree deodorizer and alcohol.

I shifted to first gear but halted with one foot on the clutch and the other on the brake.

What I was thinking was not possible. Granted, the door locks were one of the things that didn't work, but my back seat was so small, only an agile midget could hide there.

In the rearview mirror a black figure rose from the back seat, and it was no agile midget.

A cold steel blade pressed against my neck.

The scent of phony trees and alcohol surrounded me.

"Gary?" Why would Gary want that key? "What are you doing here? Your car's at the hotel."

"Who has only one car?"

Me.

"Drive."

"No!"

The blade bit into my neck.

I gulped and decided to drive. "Where?"

He hesitated. He couldn't possibly have sobered up in the hour since I'd seen him stumbling drunk at the restaurant. Maybe I could talk my way out of this.

"You haven't thought this out very well, have you?" My voice sounded a little choked. A knife at the throat will do that to you. "Maybe we should go inside and talk about it. Have a drink. I have some lovely wine." Maybe it didn't taste very good, but it was a lovely shade of pink.

The knife pressed more tightly. "Shut up and drive."

I shut up and drove.

"Turn right at the end of the street."

I turned right at the end of the street.

We came to a stop sign. "How about I give you my purse with the key Ransom gave me and the twenty dollars cash in my wallet? You get out here, and everything's fine."

"You called me Gary."

"I have no idea who you are. Gary is what I call everybody who hides in my backseat with a knife. Doesn't mean anything. Sort of like they call unidentified dead bodies John Doe." I decided to stop talking. Probably not a good idea to bring up dead bodies.

"Left on Lakeshore Drive."

Damn. The lake. Several acres of trees and hills, places a body could be hidden for years.

"Trent's waiting for me at the hospital. If I don't get there soon, he'll track me down. I have a GPS chip implanted in my arm because he's a cop and that's what they do to their girlfriends."

"Trent's at the hospital with Kathleen. He's not waiting for you."

"Yes, he is. He texted me."

"No, he didn't. I did. I took his cell phone when we were wrestling on the sidewalk. You didn't really believe I was drunk, did you?"

My heart sank to the pit of my stomach. Fred was home with his cell phone nearby in case I should call, Henry was sleeping off his bender, and Trent was at the hospital with his ex-wife. I was alone in the car with a sober man and a knife, a big knife. Gary was no longer a kid playing with a pocket knife. He and his knife had grown up.

We passed the last house before entering the woods surrounding the lake.

I was going to die.

Chapter Sixteen

But not without a fight.

If a dead body could get lost in all the trees, a live body should stand an even better chance.

I hit the gas as we approached a sharp curve and spun around the corner on two wheels. Maybe one and a half.

The knife fell away from my throat and Gary cursed.

I slid around another curve before he could recover, braced myself, and slammed on the brakes. He cursed even louder. That man has a really foul mouth.

I leapt out of the car and slammed the door behind me to make it harder for him to follow me. It would take him a few minutes to find the recessed handle, get the door open from the back seat, and struggle out. By then I should be hidden in the deep shadows of the woods.

I ran toward those woods as fast as my adrenalin powered legs would carry me. I felt a tiny bit of relief as I left the pavement and darted between trees, but the sound of leaves crunching beneath my feet was surely loud enough to lead Gary right to me. He had been a Boy Scout. I could only hope his tracking skills were as bad as his fire-making skills and not as good as his skills with a knife.

I plunged forward, stepped in a hole, gasped, cursed, and hit the ground. Running in the woods at night wasn't like running along the park trail in the afternoon. The woods were dark and deep, filled with unknown traps and horrors. What would I encounter next? Another hole? Bengal tiger trap? Big Foot? Wolfman? Dracula?

Gary and his knife were scarier.

I scrambled to my feet, put weight on the ankle, and cursed again. It hurt, but I didn't have Kathleen's option of hanging onto someone else's boyfriend's arm and going to the emergency room.

I forced myself to keep moving, to ignore the pain.

Had I gone deep enough that I could risk heading in the direction of the road?

A shot exploded through the air, the sound ricocheting through the trees.

My legs and my heart pounded faster. Did he learn to shoot in Boy Scouts too?

I thought I heard feet crunching the leaves behind me though it was hard to hear anything over my loud breathing and the hammering of my heart.

I had no idea where I was, if I was heading in the direction of the road or the lake or back to Gary.

Maybe it was time to stop and hide.

I darted behind a big oak tree that still had most of its leaves. Not that the leaves would help unless I could climb the tree. I couldn't.

I couldn't stand there and wait helplessly either. I needed a weapon to defend myself. If only I'd thought to bring along my iron skillet.

I groped through the dead leaves on the ground, hoping to find a gun some murderer had tossed there recently and hoping not to wake a hibernating snake.

I found a broken branch a couple of feet long. It would have to do.

I hefted it like a baseball bat and waited.

Footsteps.

Leaves crunching.

I peeked around the tree.

The silhouette of a male figure coming toward me.

"Lindsay?"

Even as I swung, I recognized the voice and the white hair.

Oops.

Fred raised his arm, diverting the blow from his head.

"I'm sorry!" I whispered. "Is your arm okay? Did I break your arm?"

"I'm fine, and I'm glad to see you're okay." He spoke in normal tones.

I put a hand over his mouth. "Shhh! Gary's coming after me."

He removed my hand. "No, he's not."

"Yes, he is!" I whispered. "He has a knife and a gun! He hid in my car. He was going to kill me because he smelled like an artificial tree and booze!"

Fred tilted his head. "What?"

"I mean, I recognized him so he has to kill me. He shot at me. Bullet barely missed me." I lifted a hand half an inch from the side of my head. "I think it took a couple of hairs."

"There was no gunshot. He had a knife but no gun."

"But I heard it!"

"Trent slammed your car door after he yanked Gary out. Maybe you heard that and your fear magnified it to sound like a gunshot."

"I wasn't afraid."

Fred showed he was really my friend when he didn't challenge that outrageous lie. "Let's get back to your car. Trent's worried about you."

He extended an arm toward me, the same arm he'd used to block my swing. I was relieved but not surprised to see it wasn't dangling in half. I'd always sucked at baseball.

"I'm glad your arm's okay."

"It's fine. Are you limping?"

"I stepped into a death pit lined with barbed wire and filled with snakes, fell to the hard-packed earth, and twisted my ankle."

"You've had a rough night. Would you like me to carry you?"

I wasn't sure if he was being sarcastic or serious, but no way was I going to let him pick me up and figure out how much I weighed. "Thank you for the offer, but I'm fine."

"Please allow me to hold onto your arm in case we encounter another death pit and I stumble."

"That's a good idea."

Yes, we both knew he was again allowing me to save face, but I didn't want to hurt his feelings by rejecting his offer.

He took my arm and we started back through the woods.

"How did Trent get here? How did you get here?" I scanned my arms, searching for scars. It was too dark to see anything. "Did you implant a GPS in my arm when I wasn't looking?"

"I've been following you since you left your house."

He didn't deny that he'd implanted a GPS in my arm.

"You have? How did you know I was going to leave? I wasn't planning to."

I wasn't facing Fred. I couldn't see him rolling his eyes, but I knew he was. I could hear it.

"You often act impetuously," he said. "With everything going on, I thought it best to monitor your actions. Trent lost his cell phone. I'm going to guess that had something to do with why you left."

"Gary used it to send me a text asking me to come to the hospital. I thought it was from Trent. What's he doing here? I understand you were spying on me, but how did you get hold of him? Gary has his phone."

"Watch that hole." Fred tugged me a couple of feet to the side. Night vision as well as x-ray vision. "When Trent noticed his cell phone was missing, he used Kathleen's phone to call you. You didn't answer, so he called me. I told him you'd left home and I was following you. He intersected us just as you turned down this road. When we got here, Gary was still in your back seat, searching your purse for that key. Your plan worked."'

"Yay, me."

We emerged from the woods onto the lake road. Trent's sedan was parked behind my car with Trent and Gary standing beside it.

I charged over to the two men.

"What's wrong with your ankle?" Trent asked.

I suppose my charge mode was a little lopsided. Charge, limp, curse, charge, limp, curse.

I grabbed the front of Gary's black shirt and expelled a few of the new curse words I'd learned from him. I'm pretty brave with a cop and Fred to back me up.

Gary flinched backward but made no other response.

Trent took my hand and tugged it away from Gary's shirt. "Lindsay, don't assault my prisoner."

"Prisoner?" I liked the sound of that. Gary's arms were behind his back. "Is he handcuffed?"

"Yes."

He was helpless, the way I'd been in the car. I could assault him like he'd done to me.

Except that Trent was standing beside him, watching me.

"This creep..." I jabbed a finger toward him. "This creep lured me out of my house by sending me a text message from you saying you needed me to come to the hospital. He hid in my car and he held a knife to my throat and he threatened to kill me."

Trent nodded. "I'll need you to come down and press charges. All I have on him so far is assaulting an officer and resisting arrest."

"He's guilty of murder. If you find that knife he held at my throat—"

"It's in an evidence bag in my car."

"I'll bet you find blood on it from the drug guy he murdered in my back yard after Henry ran him out of my house. Make him take off his shirt."

"What?"

"I want to see if he has scratches. Henry took a few chunks out of the man who broke into my house." Gary flinched at that accusation. I leaned closer, invading his space, my nose only inches from his. "Take off your shirt."

He stared over my shoulder.

"Lindsay," Trent said, "we'll get a warrant and do all that at the station. If you're ready to press charges against him for breaking into your car and threatening your life, we need to leave and take care of that."

I wasn't ready for this to be official. I still had questions. Things did not make sense. Gary had threatened me with a knife. The drug guy had been killed in my back yard with a knife. Ransom had been killed with a knife.

But Corey had killed Ransom.

Who had broken into my house? Corey or Gary? Were they working together? Was Kathleen the promised prize for both of them?

I folded my arms and glared at Gary. "We're going to find out tomorrow what that key guards. The Gablers found the lock it fits."

I was exaggerating a little. The Gablers found a lock it might fit. Close enough.

Gary stared straight ahead and didn't confess. In fact, he didn't even look scared at my threat to expose the contents that key guarded, the key he'd been so hot to get his hands on.

Trent took Gary's arm. "We need to go to the station now. He's invoked his right to an attorney, but I can hold him tonight if you want to go home and relax then come in tomorrow to press charges."

"I'm ready to do it now. Where's Kathleen? Has she already been arrested?" I couldn't wait to see her behind bars, wearing orange.

"Kathleen? No, she hasn't been arrested. The doctor said there was nothing wrong with her ankle so I sent her back to her hotel in a taxi and came to check on you."

I spun to face him. "She faked an injury to get you away from me so Gary could kidnap me and force me to give him that key. Corey said he killed for her. She's the master mind behind all these murders, and you sent her back to her hotel room in a taxi? You're not going to arrest the woman who almost got me killed?"

Trent stood for a moment, his dark gaze fixed on me. Then he took Gary's arm and turned away, leading him toward his car. "I have no evidence against Kathleen."

If he hadn't turned away, he would have been able to see the sparks shooting upward from my head.

No evidence? Just the word of the woman he claimed to love.

"I'm going to take you up on that offer of coming in tomorrow instead of tonight," I said.

He paused with the door to his backseat half open and looked at me.

Too late. The sparks had been replaced by ice. He wouldn't be able to see that in the cold black of the night.

"I'll go to your place as soon as I get the prisoner booked."

"Why? I'm safe now, right? Gary's in custody and all's right with the world."

Trent's eyes narrowed. "I'll be at your place in an hour."

An hour should give me enough time to get to Kathleen's hotel room and force her to confess. Fred would follow me, of course, but, short of physical violence, he couldn't stop me. I just needed to be sure he couldn't tattle on me to Trent until it was a done deal.

"Will I be able to get hold of you on your cell phone?" I was pretty sure I knew the answer.

He shook his head. "It's evidence now. I'll pick up a new one and call you when I leave the station."

"Okay."

From the corner of my vision I saw Fred stand stiffly upright. I could feel his gaze on me.

He knew what *okay* meant.

Chapter Seventeen

Trent led the procession as we drove out of the wooded area and back toward the street. I followed him and Fred followed me.

Trent turned off and headed for the police station. I turned off and headed to the Pleasant Grove Manor.

Fred stayed behind me. I drove slowly to be sure I didn't lose him. I could have done this alone, but Fred has a way of getting information out of people.

We pulled into the Pleasant Grove Manor parking lot. He parked next to me, got out, and came over to where I stood beside my car.

"Kathleen?" he asked.

I nodded. "We have to trick her into confessing and record it."

"Any idea how we do that?"

I couldn't believe he was asking me. He's always the one who comes up with ideas. "We tell her Gary's been arrested and, um, he's going to flip on her."

He shook his head.

Even I had to admit my suggestion was pretty lame. "Uh, okay, how about if we tell her we want to help her get away, but she has to tell us the truth."

I shook my head before he had a chance. "I know. That sucks. Look, I make chocolate, you come up with ways to get information out of people. So you tell me what we can do."

"You're targeting the wrong person. You want to prove to Trent that Kathleen's guilty. You're letting your emotions overrule your logic. We need to talk to Corey."

I frowned. "Corey's not going to talk to us. He knows we're not Professor Walter Keats and Elizabeth Shelby. After that visit, he probably won't say anything to us except, *Go away*."

"Let's go inside. It's cold out here."

He was right. The adrenalin from my brush with death had worn off, and I was shivering.

We went in. It was Friday night. The bar area on one side of the lobby held a few people, but it wasn't crowded. Friday night in Pleasant Grove doesn't bring out the wild partiers. Neither does Saturday night. There aren't a lot of wild partiers in Pleasant Grove.

Fred indicated an empty table in the corner.

We sat and he called someone on his cell phone.

"Mr. Paggett, this is Fred Sommers. I have a video of you and Kathleen sitting in Death by Chocolate. The audio component of that video includes a confession that you committed murder for her. Unless you want me to give that confession to the police, you need to come downstairs and talk to me. Come by yourself. Do not bring Kathleen. My assistant and I are sitting at the corner table. I'll order a martini for you." He disconnected the call.

"You lied to him."

"Not really. You have the audio and video stored in your brain." He waved to a waitress across the room.

"You can't turn my brain over to the police."

He gave me a look that made me wonder if he could.

The waitress came to our table.

"Two martinis and two glasses of your best Pinot Grigio."

Corey arrived and shoved her out of the way. His hair was still moussed and spiked in contrast to the rest of his disheveled appearance. His shirt was wrinkled and tucked half in and half out of his tight jeans. His beard looked scruffy, and his sparkling white teeth were hidden behind tightly compressed lips. He no longer looked arrogant and assured. He looked angry and terrified.

He paused with his hands on the back of the chair across from Fred. "You." The single word burst from his mouth with the force of a swear word.

"Me." Fred nodded in my direction. "And her. This time we're not playing games. This time we're serious. If you'd told us the truth the first time around, we wouldn't be here now."

Corey shook his head. "We're not here now." He turned to leave.

I started to rise from my chair. What was I planning to do? Grab him?

"We're not after you," Fred said, "but if you force us, we will use that recording to take you down."

I settled back into my chair.

Corey turned around, his brow furrowed. "If you made a recording of my conversation without my consent at a time when I had an expectation of privacy, that recording is not admissible in court."

"This isn't about going to court."

The waitress arrived and set the drinks on the table.

Corey twitched.

"Sit," Fred ordered.

He sat and gulped half the first martini.

Fred sipped his wine. "My employer wants Kathleen, not you."

Interesting. Was he referring to me as his employer? I picked up my glass of wine and leaned back to watch the Fred Show.

Corey jerked his head back and forth in a negative response. "Kathleen's not involved in anything. I don't know what you're talking about."

"I told you to come alone." Fred pointed over Corey's shoulder. "What's Kathleen doing here?"

Corey spun around to look.

So did I.

I didn't see her.

"Where?" Corey asked.

"Sorry. Not her." Fred took another sip of wine.

"Who are you and what do you want?"

"I'm Fred Sommers, and I want to know all the details of Kathleen's plot to kill her husband."

Corey drained his first martini and reached for the second. "I don't know what you're talking about."

209

"You will soon. When I diverted your attention to look for Kathleen, I put a heavy dose of drugs in both your drinks." Corey's eyes widened and he set the half-empty glass back on the table. "Don't worry. You'll be fine. The only effect will be that you'll do whatever I tell you to do, and you'll answer all my questions truthfully."

Corey's jaw went slack as panic spread over his face. He looked at me.

I smiled.

Drugs.

Go, Fred!

Fred laid a small device that looked like a flash drive on the table. He turned it on then gave the date, time, location, and our names. "Corey Paggett, do I have your permission to record our conversation?"

Corey stared at Fred as if he didn't understand the question.

Fred nodded.

Corey nodded.

"Would you please vocalize your agreement for the recorder? Do I have your permission to record this conversation? Please say the word *yes.*"

Corey nodded again. "Yes." The single word came out soft and slow as if he were drugged.

Well.

"Please tell me about your relationship with Kathleen Gabler."

"We're in love. We're going to get married."

"Was Kathleen going to divorce her husband?"

Corey moved his head slowly back and forth. "He wouldn't give her a divorce. He abused her. She was afraid he was going to kill her."

"How did you plan to resolve Kathleen Gabler's problem with her husband?"

"I promised I would kill him."

I shivered. His flat tone made the horrendous words even worse.

"Please tell me the details of your plan to murder Jeff Gabler." Fred's tone had no emotion either. He might as well have been asking Corey how he planned to get back to his room.

"We waited until he scheduled a trip to Kansas City. I came the day before he got here and checked into the Sleep-E-Z Motel as Carl Smith. She left the day after he did and drove straight to her ex-husband's house. He's a sucker and she knew he'd take her in and give her an alibi."

My hands clenched into fists on the table.

If Trent was such a sucker, maybe he'd give me an alibi after I killed Kathleen.

"What was your role in Jeff Gabler's murder?" Fred asked.

"I went to Jeff's room at two a.m. while Kathleen was with her ex-husband. I went there to kill her husband."

I bit my lip. It had to be the effect of the drug that made this man sound so unfeeling about such a contemptuous act.

"How did you get into Jeff's hotel room?"

"I knocked, but he didn't answer. Then I saw the door was open. It's an old hotel, not like those new ones that lock automatically. I went in. He was lying on the floor, dead, with blood everywhere."

"What?" The word burst from my lips before I could stop it.

Corey looked at me in surprise as if he'd forgotten I was there.

I cringed and put my hand over my mouth. Had I interrupted the flow of the truth drug?

"He was already dead when you got there?" Fred asked.

"Yes."

Corey had not killed Ransom. Fred's drug forced him to tell the truth. The confession I'd overheard was bogus.

Kathleen wasn't guilty of murder. I wasn't going to be able to visit her on death row and make fun of her orange jumpsuit.

"What did you do then?" Fred asked.

Corey shifted in his seat. "I ran. When I got back to my motel room, I texted Kathleen that the job was done."

"You let Kathleen think you killed her husband?"

"She said if I killed him, I'd be her hero, that she'd marry me."

"You and Kathleen Gabler plotted to kill her husband, but you didn't complete that plan because someone killed him before you got there?"

"If Kathleen finds out, she won't marry me."

"Do you know who killed Jeff Gabler?"

"No."

The waitress approached our table. Fred waved her away. "Where's Kathleen now?" he asked.

"In her room. We can't be seen together for a while."

Fred turned off the recorder and put it in his shirt pocket. "Lindsay, why don't you go across the lobby and call your friend while Corey and I wait here. Trent needs to know about this situation as well as the probability that Gary is the murderer."

Yes, Trent needed to know what we'd just discovered. But... "What about the..." I indicated Corey's martini glasses. "Should we destroy the evidence?"

Fred rose. "Please wait here, Corey. My assistant and I need a moment."

We walked a few feet away.

Fred leaned close to my ear. "There are no drugs."

I nodded. "Got it. No drugs. Don't worry. I won't tell Trent, but we need to get rid of the martini glasses. I'll take them with me and dump them in a trash container somewhere."

"That's not necessary. There are no drugs. I used only the power of suggestion."

I stepped back and frowned. "No drugs?"

"No drugs."

"He told us all that because of the power of suggestion? You don't have to lie to me. I'll cover for you."

"I promise, no drugs."

"So that makes you like Svengali?"

He shrugged. "Look at Corey's appearance. He's obviously susceptible to peer pressure. If my idea hadn't worked, we could always have used the cattle prods on him."

"Really?"

"No. Call Trent and get him over here." He went back to the table where Corey waited patiently, victim of the power of suggestion.

Wow.

He didn't kill Ransom. Fred thought Gary did it. Ransom had the key to something Gary wanted. He wanted that key so badly he'd broken into my house, killed the man outside, and then he'd kidnapped me.

Kathleen's story about the intruder in her hotel room was probably true.

Gary was a lawyer. He knew his rights. He wasn't going to admit to anything.

The cops might have collected enough DNA from Henry's claws to put him in my house. That might be enough to convict him of killing the drug guy standing guard outside my house.

But what evidence would they have that he killed his friend?

Finding what that key unlocked was critical.

I fumbled in my purse and brought out my cell phone. It was almost midnight. Probably too late to call the Gablers and ask to see what was in Ransom's toy chest tonight.

It might be worth it if we found a gun inside that was used to commit another murder and had Gary's fingerprints on it.

Or a head wrapped in plastic, ditto Gary's fingerprints.

Or we might find Ransom's collection of DVDs from his teenage years.

I started to call Trent but realized I didn't know his new number. I'd have to go through 911. Gary continued to cause problems.

Chapter Eighteen

Trent called me back and listened to my excited recitation of Corey's confession and Fred's recording. I left out the part about the truth serum. There was no truth serum. No reason to bring it up.

I also left out the part about Kathleen regarding him as a *sucker*. He sort of was, but I didn't want to hurt his feelings.

I waited for his reaction. I didn't expect him to be thrilled that his ex-wife had used him to establish an alibi so her lover could kill her husband.

Well, maybe I kind of did.

He wasn't.

"We'll be there in a few minutes." Cold, emotionless cop.

"Okay." I gave his attitude right back to him.

"Don't do anything until we get there."

"Okay."

He hung up.

I looked at the phone for a moment.

Don't do anything?

What did that mean? I had to do all sorts of things. Breathe in, breathe out. Swallow. Maybe go to the bathroom.

And I had to guard Kathleen and be sure she didn't leave the hotel until Trent got there to arrest her.

I walked back over to where Fred and Corey waited. Corey still appeared to be in a daze.

I believed Fred when he said there were no drugs involved. He never lies to me. Often he doesn't answer a question, but he never lies to me.

He must have used the Vulcan Mind Meld.

I'd ask him later, and he'd probably not answer me later.

"Trent's on his way," I said.

"Good."

"And I need to go upstairs and wait outside Kathleen's room to be sure she doesn't escape."

He looked at me for a long moment then nodded. "You want to see her hauled out in handcuffs."

"Yes."

"All right, but wait down the hall and call me if she starts to leave. Don't do anything."

Why was everybody obsessed with me not doing anything?

I rode the shaky, ancient elevator to the fourth floor and strode down the hallway to room 413. It was halfway between the stairs and the elevator. Fred had instructed me to wait down the hall. That wasn't possible with two exits to block.

I took my position directly across the hall from her room, took out my cell phone, and activated the camera. *See her in handcuffs?* I wanted a picture of her in handcuffs.

Her door looked ordinary, the same as the other ones that lined the hallway. Nothing unique about hers except the number.

What did I expect? What did a door hiding a wanna-be murderer look like? Flames shooting out the keyhole? Blood trickling from inside or spelling out *Redrum* on the door?

None of the above.

I waited.

And waited.

What was taking so long? It was a small town. Trent was at the station a few miles away when I talked to him.

I checked my watch. It had only been ten minutes.

Finally the elevator doors opened and Gerald Lawson stepped out first.

And last.

"Where's Trent?"

"Downstairs." He strode to Kathleen's door and knocked. "Police."

I opened my mouth to protest then closed it. I didn't want to see Lawson drag Kathleen off to jail. I wanted to see Trent do it. I wanted to know that he could do it, that he…

I bit my lip. I wanted to know that he wasn't still in love with her.

I didn't want to think that. I wanted to believe I was only waiting to photograph Kathleen hauled away in handcuffs so I could gloat.

But the awful truth was, I needed to know Trent could do it. And that wasn't going to happen.

Kathleen answered the door. She wore a red silk gown. Her hair and makeup were immaculate.

She was expecting someone.

Gary?

Corey?

Trent?

Lawson flashed his badge. "Kathleen Gabler, you're under arrest for conspiracy to commit murder."

She stepped backward and tried to close the door.

Lawson lifted an arm and held the door open. "You have the right to remain silent. Anything you say can and will be used against you in a court of law."

Kathleen's gaze narrowed to evil slits. "How dare you? Get away from my door." She tried again to close it.

Lawson maintained his hold with no apparent effort. "You have the right to an attorney. If you cannot afford an attorney—"

"I know my rights. My husband is an attorney."

Is? Was or *will be* would have been more accurate.

"—one will be provided for you. Would you like to change clothes before we leave?"

"Detective Adam Trent is a friend of mine. I demand to see him."

"Yes, ma'am. He's downstairs. If you'd like to change into warmer clothes, we can go downstairs."

Kathleen lifted her chin. "I need privacy to change clothes."

Lawson stepped back and released his hold on her door.

She disappeared into the room.

A couple of minutes later my cell phone rang, a number I didn't recognize.

Trent. "You need to come downstairs."

"But—"

"Kathleen is not going to come out of the room as long as you're there."

That woman had seen me and snitched me off. She'd called Trent. And Trent was doing what she wanted.

"I'm on my way," I ground out through gritted teeth.

I headed for the stairs. I didn't want to ride the elevator. I didn't want to stand passively in a box. I stomped down each step all the way to the lobby.

Actually, I was so busy stomping I missed the door to the lobby and stomped my way to the basement. I had to turn around and stomp back to the main floor.

By the time I got to the lobby, all I saw was Trent's back as he ushered Corey through the front door to a squad car parked at the curb. Trent put him in the backseat then got in the passenger side in front. Lawson must be driving. Kathleen must be seated in the other side of the backseat, a position where I couldn't see her.

Damn!

They drove away.

Double damn!

Fred came up behind me. "You should go home and get some sleep. You look tired."

Tired?

As the anger drained, I realized I was tired. Exhausted. Emotionally and physically.

I nodded. "Good idea."

ᖇᖇ

Being tired doesn't necessarily lead to sleep.

I tossed, turned, dozed, tossed, turned…

Henry lifted his head and glowered at me. I was interrupting his sleep.

Shortly after 2:00 a.m. I heard the front door open.

I sat bolt upright in bed. Had Gary somehow made bail in the middle of the night and come back for that key?

At the foot of my bed Henry raised his head, gave me a disgusted look, and leapt to the floor where he curled up and went back to sleep.

Henry wasn't excited. I had no cause to be excited.

Footsteps came up the stairs.

I grabbed my iron skillet from the nightstand.

"Did I wake you?" Trent asked.

I laid the skillet back on the nightstand. "No." My voice croaked a little since my heart was still in my throat.

"I'm sorry. I probably shouldn't have come over this late."

I lifted the covers. "I'm glad you did."

He climbed in and pulled me close. "I was so worried about you." He pulled me even closer. "I'm the one in the dangerous profession. I catch criminals. You make chocolate. You're supposed to worry whether I'll get hurt, but I have to worry about you because somebody's always breaking in or kidnapping you or trying to kill you. Get your car locks fixed. Get your garage fixed. Get metal doors on your house. I love you. I can't live without you. I need you to be safe."

It was the most impassioned speech I'd ever heard him make, and it went a long way toward relieving my fears about Kathleen. I wanted to ask how he felt about the fact that she'd planned to kill his friend, but I didn't want to bring her into our world. I wanted to savor the time between us.

First I had to tell him about my conversation with the Gablers and the possibility that the infamous key might fit the lock on Ransom's toy chest. "I told them we'd be over around 4:30 or 5:00, but I assume your meeting with Kathleen and Gary is off since they're both in jail. We can probably go as soon as I close up. I'll call them in the morning and set a definite time. What works for you? Around 3:00?"

"That's okay. I'll call them. Since I have the key, it's official police business."

Trent's body was warm against mine, his breathing slow and intimate. He loved me. He worried about me. Kathleen was in jail.

I didn't want to disrupt the closeness.

Therefore I refrained from pointing out to him that Ransom had left the key for me to find and that his parents had called me.

I would be there when that toy chest was opened, official police business or unofficial Lindsay business.

Chapter Nineteen

As usual Paula was rolling out dough when I got to work the next morning. "How was your evening with Trent and his high school buddy?"

I grabbed an apron. "You're not going to believe it."

She continued rolling. "Yes, I will."

I tied the apron strings behind me. "If I have to leave for half an hour today, can you cover for me?"

"It depends. Are you planning to do something that involves Kathleen? You've become a little obsessed with her."

"She's in jail."

Paula's rolling pin halted halfway across the dough, and she looked up. "In jail?"

I took down my mixing bowl and made cookies while I told her about Fred's ruse and Corey's confession.

She showed no surprise.

When I told her about Gary holding a knife to my throat, she gasped and lifted a hand to her throat. "You need to get your garage repaired and park your car in it."

"I'm going to get my car repaired and painted and then I'll get the garage fixed."

"More like burn it down and start all over."

"My garage?"

"No. Your car."

I let that one pass. She'd change her mind when she saw my car all shiny and dentless.

"Do you think normal people are awake yet?" I asked.

We opened for brunch on Saturday. The hour was later than usual, but it was still dark outside.

"Not this early. Why do you ask?"

"I need to call the Gablers but I don't want to wake them."

"Give it a few hours."

"I'll call Fred. He never sleeps."

He answered. "Do you know what time it is?"

"Of course I know. Don't you? Is your clock broken?" Another thought struck me. "Is Sophie there?" I cringed at the idea that I might have interrupted something.

"I assume you have some reason for calling me at this hour."

"Were you sleeping?"

"I was."

"Oh. I'm sorry. We need to get an appointment as soon as possible to take the copy you have of that key to the Gablers and see if it opens Ransom's toy chest."

Silence.

"Are you still awake?"

"Yes. Can you explain why I need to open Ransom's toy chest?"

"Sorry. We were so busy last night, I didn't get a chance to tell you. Maggie Gabler called and said Ransom's toy chest has a new padlock on it, and she wants us to bring over the key and see if fits that lock. Gary's a lawyer. He's never going to confess, but we know he killed Ransom, and that toy chest may contain evidence to convict him."

"Shouldn't Trent be the one to open it? He has the original key, and he has legal authority to do something with any evidence that may be in the box."

"I was going to let him go with us, but he says that toy chest is official police business. He'll open it and never tell me what was in it."

"I see. Maybe we could all go together."

"When he gets on that police kick, you can't reason with him."

"Let me try."

"Call me back."

"I will, but not soon. Trent's car is still at your house and I assume the Gablers are sound asleep as are most people in this time zone."

He hung up.

The day got busy fast, so busy I didn't have time to bug Fred every few minutes about our visit to the Gablers. But I had plenty of time to worry about it and wonder if Trent and Lawson had already been there and discovered the contents of that toy chest and I'd never, ever know what was in it because it was official police business.

Fred finally called a few minutes after 1:00, just as I locked the door behind the last customer.

"Three o'clock," he said. "You, me, Trent, and Lawson."

"Are you bringing your copy of the key?"

"Not unless you want to tell your boyfriend that I made one."

"Not really."

"Come home first, and you and I can ride over there together."

"So you can keep an eye on me and be sure I don't *do anything*?"

He hung up.

❧❦

The neighborhood where Trent and his friends grew up had towering trees and large lawns with small, tidy houses. The older area had aged gracefully.

Fred stopped in front of a white house with green shutters and door. Three large pine trees loomed from the back yard. They had survived the ill-fated experiment with a cigarette lighter.

We walked down the sidewalk to the front porch.

"I don't see Trent's car," I said. "If by any chance you have that duplicate key in your pocket…"

"We'll wait for Trent."

"Of course. I was just asking."

Rats.

Maggie Gabler opened the front door as soon as we stepped onto the porch. Lines etched her face and she looked several years older than the day before. "Good to see you again, Lindsay. And you must be Fred."

Fred stepped forward and shook her hand.

"Come in. I've made a fresh pot of coffee."

I gave her a hug. I'm not really a hugger, but the occasion seemed to call for it.

She hugged me back tightly. "I'm so glad you're okay."

"You heard what happened last night?"

Her lips thinned. "Gary was my son's friend, and Kathleen was my son's wife. I don't understand how they…" She lifted a hand to her lips.

I held up the box of desserts I'd brought and forced a smile. "I have chocolate."

She returned my smile even though her eyes were shiny with tears. "Chocolate always helps."

We went inside.

Warren Gabler introduced himself to Fred. "Have a seat. Adam's on his way."

Warren looked as tired as his wife.

The living room was cozy and inviting with comfortably worn furniture, lots of pictures, and a brick fireplace with bookshelves on both sides.

Maggie brought coffee and Coke along with a large glass plate for my chocolate offerings and a stack of matching dessert plates.

In the cozy, comfortable room we all settled uncomfortably. Fred and I sat on the sofa, Maggie and Warren on the loveseat. Actually Fred never seems uncomfortable, not even when somebody's trying to kill him or bash him with a tree branch. But the rest of us did.

"It's so hard to take in," Maggie said. "Jeff was a good person. Everyone loved him. I knew he and Kathleen had their problems. I didn't like her, didn't like the way she treated him, but I would never have dreamed she'd want to kill him."

"Kathleen is evil and devious." I wasn't a bit prejudiced.

Maggie dabbed her eyes with a tissue. "I liked Gary when he was a little boy. I felt sorry for him. He was a late in life baby, and he could never measure up to his older brothers. They were honor students and athletes. For the most part, his parents ignored him. The only thing he and his dad did together was deer hunting."

"I guess that explains his obsession with knives." I would never forget the feel of that cold blade pressed against my neck. "If he can skin a buck, he can slit somebody's throat."

"I don't know if I'm hoping we find nothing but dusty old toys in Jeff's chest or evidence to prove who murdered our son," Maggie said.

If the key Gary wanted badly enough to kill for it fit the padlock on Ransom's toy chest, the contents would likely incriminate him. That was my optimistic assumption.

For once, I kept my mouth shut. No need to add to Maggie's sadness until we knew something definite.

Warren wrapped an arm around his wife's shoulders. "It's hard enough to deal with losing Jeff, but to think the kids who played in our yard and ate at our table may have been involved..." He choked and held his wife closer.

I nibbled on a brownie which had changed from moist and chewy to dry and tasteless between one bite and the next. Suddenly I wasn't so anxious to see the contents of that toy chest.

Someone knocked on the door.

Maggie and Warren went to the door. Trent came in, embraced Maggie, and he and Warren did the man hug thing.

Lawson walked in behind Trent.

They did introductions, but nobody hugged Lawson. I considered doing it just so he'd feel included, but the stony expression on his face discouraged me.

Maggie offered coffee and chocolate to the new arrivals.

Trent ran his hands down the legs of his jeans and cleared his throat. "Do you want to wait or do this now?"

"Now." Maggie's voice was firm.

Trent produced the key. "This may be a false alarm. It may not fit."

Nobody believed that.

Maggie and Warren led us down the hall to a back bedroom.

The twin size bed, small desk, and white wooden chest in the corner identified it as a child's room, that of a boy who, through the years, had probably changed the bed spread from cartoon characters to super heroes to the current masculine dark plaid.

The wooden chest with a shiny new padlock was roughly the size of a trunk and could hold a lot of toys and video games, perhaps law books during college, and now...?

The six of us huddled in the room, looking at the chest but not moving toward it. Macabre visions of severed heads, bloody hammers, and deadly guns alternated with visions of stuffed dogs, toy trucks, and baseball gloves.

Trent squeezed my hand then reached inside his jacket pocket, withdrew a small envelope, and produced the key then donned rubber gloves.

His hazel eyes were so dark, I could barely distinguish the pupils.

He was a cop, through and through. But Ransom had been his friend. He was, as he'd said, personally involved.

He crossed the room, knelt beside the chest, and inserted the key.

The padlock opened.

The air in the room became preternaturally still and silent.

I held my breath.

Nobody moved.

Finally, slowly, he lifted the lid.

From across the room I stared at the contents.

Books, DVDs, video games, odds and ends of the life of a boy grown into a man. No severed head. No bloody hammer.

I dared to breathe again.

Trent took out a book and laid it on the floor, then a DVD and a video game. Finally he produced a large brown envelope with the word *Private* sprawled across it in bold red letters.

He held up the envelope and looked at Maggie and Warren.

Maggie bit her lip and nodded.

"Open it. Now." Warren's voice cracked when he spoke.

Lawson, also wearing gloves, crossed the room and stood beside Trent.

Trent rose and withdrew the contents of the envelope.

Papers and pictures.

A small card fell to the floor.

A driver's license.

Trent retrieved it.

The top paper was a typed document. He and Lawson looked it for several moments then lifted it to expose pictures. From my distance I couldn't see the details of the pictures. Trent and Lawson scanned them and handed them back and forth but did not offer to share.

I had to know. I took a step toward Trent and Lawson. Fred laid a hand on my arm. "Wait," he said softly.

I didn't want to wait any longer. I wanted to read that document and see those pictures. I wanted to know what had been so important that Gary was willing to kill me to get it.

This was like being stuck at one of those traffic lights so long that people begin with teen-age acne and end up on social security before it changes.

"What does it say?" I asked. "Who's in the pictures?" Somebody had to break the spell.

Trent lifted a troubled gaze to mine and shook his head.

"Read it." Maggie's voice was surprisingly firm.

Trent looked at the top paper again and compressed his lips. "It's evidence."

"I call *bull*," I said. "It's not like anybody wants to touch it or change it. Read it!"

His gaze moved to me then to Lawson then to Maggie. "Let's go back to the living room and sit down."

That did not sound good.

Silently we all moved to the living room and resumed our seats.

Trent eased into the big recliner at one end of the room.

Lawson paused beside him and extended his hand. "I'll do it."

"No. I need to."

Lawson nodded then moved to the arm chair at the other end of the room.

Trent turned the pictures upside down on the lamp table beside him and clutched the printed document in both hands.

"It's dated two weeks ago." He cleared his throat. "*To whom it may concern. A year ago I, Jeffrey Gabler, came to Kansas City to spend a week taking care of some business at our main office. I came early to spend the weekend with friends and family.*" I'd heard Trent sound like a stern cop, a considerate friend, and an excited lover. This was different. His voice was a monotone, all emotion damped down far below the surface. "*At that time I was a practicing alcoholic. My friend, Gary Durant, and I went out drinking that Saturday night. Our expressed intention was to become intoxicated. By the end of the evening, we had achieved that goal.*"

Trent paused and drew in a deep breath then returned his gaze to the document. "*We were in Gary's car. We closed down the bar, bought a six-pack, and decided to go to the lake and do some moonlight fishing. At that hour, there shouldn't have been any traffic out there. But there was. A woman came out of the darkness. Gary didn't stop in time. We hit her.*"

Somebody gasped. It might have been Maggie. It might have been me.

Ransom had told me he was a former alcoholic, but I hadn't pictured him inebriated and out of control.

"*I checked on her. She was dead. I started to call 911, but Gary stopped me. We were driving under the influence. We killed a woman. We would go to prison. We would lose our law licenses. Our lives would be over.*"

Ransom had continued to practice law. He had not gone to prison. I glanced at Maggie. Her eyes were wide and wet. She was thinking the same thing I was thinking.

"*God help me, I listened to him. I knew it was wrong, but I justified my behavior by telling myself she was dead. Nothing else could be done for her.*"

Across the room Maggie sobbed softly and Warren pulled her close.

"*The woman's car was sitting a few hundred feet down the road with a flat tire. She must have been trying to flag us down when we killed her. Her purse was in her car. Gary told me to destroy all her identification while he drove the car into the lake. I couldn't do it. I saved the license so I could let her family know. While Gary was getting rid of the car, I took pictures of the body. I am enclosing the driver's license and the pictures of the body. I didn't plan it, but the pictures include the image of Gary's front license plate. I'm ashamed to admit that I never contacted that woman's family. I was afraid of being caught. We dragged her body into the woods and left her."*

A chill shot down my spine. How close had I come to the same fate as that woman…murdered and my body dragged into the woods to be left as a feast for the critters?

"I stopped drinking. If I hadn't been drunk that night, Joanna Wilkins would still be alive. That was her name, the woman we killed. I have lived with the horror of that night ever since, and I can't do it any longer. I am planning to turn myself in. I filed for divorce so Kathleen won't be the wife of a convicted felon. Our marriage has not been good, but I've already destroyed one life. I don't want to destroy another."

If I'd had any doubts that Kathleen had lied about the spousal abuse, those words would have erased that doubt. While he'd been working to protect her, she'd been plotting his murder.

"I retrieved the evidence from my safe deposit box in St. Louis, came to Kansas City and locked it in the file cabinet in my office here so it would be readily available when I went to the authorities. My confession would also convict Gary, so I met with him and told him what I planned to do. He tried to

talk me out of it. He doesn't want to lose his house, his Cadillac and Corvette, his good life. Finally he agreed. However, he then asked for the key to my file cabinet. He said he wanted to study the evidence as any lawyer would so he would be prepared."

The key had unlocked Ransom's toy chest. Had Gary thought the key was to the file cabinet?

"I let him examine everything but refused to give him the key. I want to trust him, but I want to remove temptation. Before I leave this office, I will retrieve all the evidence, buy a padlock, and move everything to my old toy chest. I will then return to St. Louis, take care of some details, and come back here in a week. I do not anticipate any problems, but should something happen to prevent me from taking this evidence to the proper authorities, Mom, Dad, or whoever finds this letter, please take the enclosed to Adam Trent. Even though Kathleen and I betrayed him, I know I can trust him to do the right thing."

Trent exhaled a long breath. "That's all."

A loud, dark silence settled over the once comfortable room.

Maggie was the first to break it. She rose and wiped her eyes. "I'll get some more coffee. Lindsay, would you like another Coke?"

I understood what she was doing. When you hurt so badly you can't face the pain, fall back on manners, beverages, and food.

"Yes, thank you." I picked up the plate of chocolate chip cookies and brownies and moved around the room.

Fred selected a cookie.

Trent hesitated.

"Take a brownie," I said. "Eat it. Don't make me force it down your throat."

He smiled.

Of course I was kidding.

Kind of.

He pulled off the rubber gloves and chose a brownie with chocolate chips and nuts.

I bullied everybody, including myself, into having some chocolate.

Maggie returned with coffee and Coke.

Warren, fortified with chocolate and caffeine, stood and walked over to the lamp table.

Trent held out a restraining hand. "It's evidence."

"My son is dead because of those pictures. I need to see them."

Trent shook his head. "No, you don't."

"A little boy who played in my yard and ate at my dinner table murdered my son. I need to see why."

Trent pulled on the rubber gloves and lifted first the small driver's license then the pictures, one at a time.

"Is it enough to convict him of killing my son?" Warren asked.

"I don't know. He'll go to prison. We'll get him for abducting Lindsay and threatening to kill her. This—" He waved a hand at Ransom's letter and the photographs. "This should be enough to convict him of Joanna Wilkins' accidental death and then covering up the crime. We're going to do a DNA match of the man who broke into Lindsay's house and murdered the drug dealer standing guard outside. We'll probably be able to get him on that. We can charge him with Jeff's murder, but the only evidence we have for that is circumstantial. He'll have a good lawyer. Whatever happens, I promise you he will go to prison for the rest of his life."

Warren's jaw firmed. "I want him to admit he killed my son."

"I don't think that's going to happen. He's a lawyer. He knows how the game is played. He's never going to confess."

I turned to look at Fred.

He looked back at me, his expression blank as if he didn't know what I was thinking.

"Fred can do it. He can get a confession." Drugs, cattle prods, Vulcan Mind Meld. I refrained from mentioning any of his methods. Despite rumors to the contrary, I can keep a secret.

"No," Fred and Trent said at the same time.

"Gary won't meet with Fred," Trent said.

"We can put Fred in disguise as a felon in jail with Gary and he'll have to meet with him."

"No!" Fred and Trent again.

"Let me talk to him." Warren's voice was soft, gentle even. Yet it gave me chills. The quiet words didn't mask the pain and anger.

"I'll talk to him," Trent said. "I don't know if I can get anything out of him. If I do, it will have to be in an unofficial capacity, off the record. I'll promise him it won't be used in court, that it will be strictly so his friend's grieving parents can find some closure."

Chapter Twenty

I left the remaining desserts with Ransom's parents. I wanted to do more for them. Make them a Death by Chocolate Cheesecake or a Triple Chocolate Mousse Cake. Do something to ease their pain.

As I hugged them good-bye on their front porch, I knew their pain went too deep for even chocolate to heal. But it would help.

Trent and Lawson drove away in their anonymous dark sedan, and Fred and I left in his immaculate white Mercedes.

"Why won't you do it?" I asked as soon as he pulled away from the curb. "Why won't you go down and make Gary confess? Maggie and Warren need to know for sure."

He turned a corner, keeping all four wheels on the street. "First, I do not believe Gary is as suggestible as Corey, and second, he'd never agree to see me. As a prisoner, he has the right to decide who he talks to. Trent has the best chance. He can appeal to their history as friends and remind Gary of the kind things the Gablers did for him when he was a boy."

"That would require that Gary have some remnant of humanity left. I don't believe he does. If Trent fails, will you try?"

He rolled his eyes.

I read somewhere that rolling our eyes is good for the eye muscles. All my friends must have very strong eye muscles.

"All right. I promise to try if Trent fails."

That was easy.

Too easy?

When we got home, I walked straight from Fred's driveway to Paula's house to tell her about the letter and pictures.

Zach and Paula were in the front yard, rolling a large colorful ball back and forth between them. Zach chased it with the energy and focus only a three year old could have. He saw me, dropped the ball, and charged over. "Anlinny! We're going to have hamburgers for dinner. You can eat with us. Mama said she needs to go inside and cook. Will you play ball with me?"

A year ago he'd have lifted his arms to be picked up. Now he was too big for that…physically and emotionally. I wished he would anyway. I wanted to hold him close and protect him from all the evil in the world.

That was, of course, impossible. One day he'd grow up and leave home, get married to some woman who didn't deserve him and be on his own.

The way Ransom had done.

"I need to talk to your mother for a few minutes. Then I'll play ball with you while she cooks dinner." Playing ball was way down on the list of things I wanted to do that Saturday afternoon, but I'd just seen how easily a son could be taken from his family. I'd play ball with Zach or whatever he wanted to do.

"Did you bring cookies? Mama says I can't have a cookie till after I eat dinner."

"No, I gave my cookies to somebody who needed them."

His small face fell. "I need cookies now."

I ruffled his blond hair. "You're tough. You can make it for a couple more hours without a cookie."

Paula joined us. "Aunt Lindsay's right. You'll survive. Why don't you come inside and play with Gordon while Aunt Lindsay and I talk?"

I followed her onto the porch. "Gordon?"

"His imaginary friend."

We all went inside. Zach grabbed an orange truck and began running in circles with it.

I followed Paula into the kitchen. I sat at the table and she put hamburger patties into a skillet.

"Zach has an imaginary friend? Do you worry about him being an only child?" Ransom had been an only child. "Have you and Matthew talked about…you know…things like marriage and children?" Even though she was my best friend, Paula didn't tell me everything the way I told her everything. Okay, I tell everybody everything. Paula's always had secrets. I don't understand that.

"No," she said. Just like that. *No*. No details. "Tell me what happened today. Did the key unlock Ransom's toy chest?"

"Yes." I thought about stopping with a one-word answer the way she had. But I couldn't. I told her everything.

She turned the hamburger patties in silence. "Are you staying for dinner?"

"No. Thanks for the offer, but I want to be home when Trent gets there."

"Please let me know if he learns anything from Gary."

"I will."

"Let's tell Zach you'll play ball with him another time. It's getting late, and dinner's almost ready."

I nodded. With her evil ex in prison, Paula had become less fearful and no longer lived in a fortress, but this reminder of how easily someone could lose a son had probably sent her back into protective mode.

Does anyone ever completely recover from the presence of evil in their lives?

Zach readily agreed to the change of ball game plans. He and Gordon were having a race with toy cars. To my intense relief, Gordon's car didn't move as Zach pushed his across the finish line.

I left and Paula closed the door behind me. I felt certain she also locked both deadbolts.

Henry joined me as I crossed the yard to my house. He was fearless. He'd never encountered an evil he couldn't take down.

I wanted to lift him into my arms and hold him close, but he would no more tolerate that than Zach would.

We went inside. He ate cat food with a side of tuna. I took a long, hot shower.

Then I got a Coke, sat on the sofa, and picked up my book.

After I read the same page three times and still had no idea what it said, I gave up on that idea.

Outside the evening shadows gathered.

Henry went to the front door and stood looking at it. He wanted to go out.

He went out every night unless it was raining or snowing.

Tonight I didn't want him to go out. I wanted him to stay inside so I could watch over him.

He stood on his back legs, front paws wrapping around the door knob, trying to turn it.

"What if you run into a coyote out there?" I asked. "What if someone tries to kidnap you?"

He dropped back onto all four feet and turned to gaze at me with those piercing blue eyes. I could read his mind. *Pity the coyote. Pity the potential kidnapper.*

"But there are other terrors in the night."

He continued to stare at me. *Pity the woman who tries to keep me inside.*

I opened the door and let him out then returned to sit on the sofa and sip my Coke while the night came inside and gathered around me.

Where was Trent? Why hadn't he called? How long did visiting hours at the jail last?

The burst of music from my cell phone startled me.

I answered.

Trent.

"I'm leaving the Gablers' house and heading your way," he said.

"Did Gary talk?"

"I'll see you in a few minutes."

How many is *a few*?

More than *a couple*.

Fewer than *a lot.*

The earth slowed. Time crawled.

Trent turned his key in the lock and came through my door seven minutes later, but it felt more like seventy.

He closed the door, came over and kissed me. "Why are you sitting in the dark?"

I flipped on the lamp beside the sofa. "Saving energy."

"I could use a beer."

I went to the refrigerator and brought back two beers and a glass of wine. "Neither of us is driving anywhere tonight. As long as we can make it upstairs, we'll be okay."

"If we can't make it upstairs, we can both sleep on the sofa."

"I get to be on top."

"Deal." He opened a can of beer and drank from it.

I drank about a fourth of my glass of wine. "Well? Did he confess?"

Trent nodded and had another long pull from his beer. He leaned forward and rested his elbows on his knees, his gaze straight ahead. "He says he didn't intend to kill Jeff. He just wanted to get the key to the file cabinet so he could destroy the evidence. He didn't want to lose everything and go to prison. He was desperate. Jeff refused to give him the key so he stabbed him."

Was he really taking up for Gary? "He just happened to have a knife with him?"

"He searched Jeff's body and the room but didn't find the key. He took Jeff's watch and wallet so it would look like a burglary, but he refused to tell me what he did with them." He spoke in a staccato tone, more emotionless than when he'd read Ransom's letter. "Kathleen was in town. He thought she might have it. He broke into her hotel room. She told him you had the key. He didn't know who you were, so he invited her to visit him and tell him about you. That's the night you followed her. She told him who you were and that Jeff had come by to see you. So he came to your house." Trent drained the rest of his beer and popped the top on the second one. "He was breaking in here when a man came out of the bushes and attacked him. He killed him. This one was self-defense. Not his fault. And, come to find out, the man was a drug dealer, so that murder shouldn't count against him either."

"*Shouldn't count against him?* So if Henry hadn't attacked him that night would he have come upstairs and murdered me when I couldn't give him the key and justified that murder too? If he'd slit my throat and dragged my body into the woods for the coyotes and worms, would that not count against him either?"

Trent finished his second beer and I downed the rest of my wine.

"I thought he'd tell me the truth because he regretted what he'd done and would want to give Jeff's parents any peace they can find. But he didn't.

He thinks everything he did was justifiable. If the woman hadn't jumped in front of his car, he wouldn't have hit her. If Jeff hadn't threatened to go to the police, everything would be fine. Jeff would still be alive, and Gary wouldn't be in custody. If the man guarding your house hadn't attacked him, he wouldn't have had to kill him."

"If he'd killed me, how would he have justified that?"

Trent shook his head slowly. "I'm sure he'd have come up with something. He killed Jeff and the drug dealer and tried to kill you to get his hands on a key that wouldn't have helped him. The key didn't fit the file cabinet. The documents weren't in the file cabinet. It was all for nothing. I grew up with Gary, played with him, went to school with him, but I didn't know him."

"How did the Gablers take it?"

"Hard. We all hung out with them so much when we were growing up, they feel like they've lost two sons. I'm going to stay in touch with them. I'm the only one of their boys they have left."

I picked up his empty cans and my empty glass and went to the kitchen to get refills.

When I returned and offered him another beer, he shook his head. "What I need right now is to hold you."

"That works for me." I snuggled up next to him on the sofa.

Ransom's murderer was in jail.

Trent's former wife was in jail.

All was right with the world.

245

Except it wasn't.

If Kathleen was free, would he be snuggling with her right now instead of me?

She wasn't free, and he was with me. I should celebrate. Let the past go.

But I had to know.

"What about Kathleen?"

He stiffened. "What about her?"

"How do you feel about what she did, planning the murder of your friend?"

"I really don't want to talk about her right now."

I pulled away and faced him. "I do. I need to know how you feel about her. You grew up with her too. You played with her. You went to school with her. You married her, and she left you for another man. Are you still in love with her?"

He put his face in his hands and for a moment I thought he was crying.

My heart clenched into a cold, hard knot.

He lifted his head and I realized he was laughing.

"It's not funny," I said.

He sobered. "No, it's not funny. It's sad. I'm not proud of myself."

His words were not what I wanted to hear.

I started to rise. "I get it."

He took my arm and restrained me from leaving. "No, you don't. I never wanted to admit this, especially not to you. But I will. Please sit down. You need to hear this." He sighed. "And I guess I need to say it."

I pulled my arm free. Suddenly I didn't want to hear what he had to say. "You don't need to say it. I don't need to hear it."

"Yes, you do. I let Kathleen stay in my apartment and put up with a lot from her because I felt guilty."

"Guilty of what? Being with me?"

"No. Guilty of being a lousy husband. I married her because she told me she was pregnant. She wasn't, but by the time I figured that out, we were married. I didn't love her. Maybe if I'd loved her...but I didn't. And then she told me she was in love with Jeff and wanted a divorce."

"And you didn't want somebody else to have her?" I guessed.

He laughed again, a dead, hollow sound. "I was so relieved to be rid of her, I didn't try to salvage our marriage, and I didn't warn Jeff about her. Then when I thought she killed him—"

I sat upright and glared at him. "You thought she killed him? No, *I* thought she killed him. You wouldn't listen to me!"

"I did listen. I was in a bad spot. She was my ex-wife. I desperately wanted to find proof that she killed Jeff, and that meant I shouldn't be involved in the case. I needed to step back and let Lawson handle it. That was hard, and then I had to worry about you provoking her and becoming a victim too. Keeping you from getting in the middle of things was even harder. You are probably the most stubborn person I've ever known."

"Not probably. Definitely. And you'd do well not to forget it."

"I won't forget that if you swear you will never forget how much I love you. Just you. Only you. After that debacle of a marriage with Kathy, I never expected to have a normal relationship. I never expected to be in love."

I fell into his lap and pressed my lips to his. He was right. I had needed to hear what he had to say.

THE END

(Keep reading for some of Lindsay's favorite recipes!)

RECIPES

Chocolate Caramel Shortbread

Preheat oven to 350 degrees. Grease 9x9 inch pan and dust with flour.

Shortbread:

1 1/4 cups flour
1/4 cup sugar
2/3 cup butter, room temperature

Combine flour and sugar. Cut in butter until it forms a crumb mixture. Press into pan and bake for 20 minutes. Remove from oven and allow to cool.

Caramel:

1/2 cup butter
1/2 cup dark brown sugar
1/2 cup sweetened condensed milk
2 Tbsp. corn syrup

Melt butter. Stir in brown sugar, corn syrup, and sweetened condensed milk. Bring to a boil and cook for 5 minutes, stirring constantly. Remove from heat and stir an additional 2 minutes or until it starts to thicken. Pour over cooled shortbread bars. Allow to cool.

Chocolate topping:

2 cups chocolate chips
1 tsp. oil

Heat chocolate chips and oil in microwave in 15
second intervals until chocolate is melted. Pour over
caramel layer and allow to set. Once chocolate has
hardened, cut into squares with a warm knife.

Chocolate Bundt Cake with Cream Cheese Filling

Preheat oven to 350 degrees.
Grease a Bundt pan and dust with cocoa.

Filling:
8 ounces cream cheese, room temperature
1/2 cup sugar
1 egg
1 tsp. vanilla
1 Tbsp. flour
    Beat cream cheese and sugar until well mixed.
Add egg, vanilla, and flour and beat again. Set aside.

Cake:
3/4 cup cocoa
3/4 cup bittersweet chocolate chips
3/4 cup hot water
1-3/4 cups flour
1/4 tsp. salt
1 tsp. baking soda
1 cup sour cream, room temperature
3/4 cup (1-1/2 sticks) butter, room temperature
2 cups dark brown sugar
1 Tbsp. vanilla
5 eggs, room temperature
    Heat water in microwave for one minute. Pour over chocolate chips and cover. Let stand 5 minutes.
    Stir together flour, cocoa, salt, and baking soda. Mix well with a fork, getting out all lumps and insuring mixture is smooth and a consistent color.

Whisk chocolate chips mixture until smooth. Let cool to room temperature. Whisk in sour cream.

Beat butter, brown sugar, and vanilla until light and fluffy. Add eggs, one at a time. Gradually add flour mixture and chocolate mixture alternatively. Beat until smooth, but do not overbeat.

Pour half the batter into Bundt pan and press it toward edges and center of pan, making a little trench. Pour cheesecake filling into the trench, keeping it away from the edges. Pour the remaining batter over the filling.

Bake for one hour or until a toothpick comes out with moist crumbs. Let cool on a rack for 10 minutes then turn the cake out and let cool completely.

Glaze:
1/2 cup cream
2 tsp. corn syrup
3/4 cup semi-sweet chocolate chips

Heat cream and corn syrup in microwave in 30 second increments until hot. Add chocolate chips and whisk until smooth. Let cool slightly until thickened. Drizzle over cake.

Raspberry Chocolate Bundt Cake

Preheat oven to 350 degrees. Grease a 10 inch Bundt pan and dust with cocoa.

1 package dark chocolate cake mix
1 (3.9 ounce) package instant chocolate fudge pudding mix
2 cups sour cream
3 eggs
1/3 cup vegetable oil
1/2 cup Chambord raspberry liqueur
2 cups chocolate chips

Combine cake mix, pudding mix, sour cream, eggs, oil, and raspberry liqueur in a mixing bowl. Beat until well blended. Fold in chocolate chips. Batter will be thick. Spoon into prepared pan.

Bake for 1 hour or until cake springs back when lightly tapped. Cool 10 minutes in pan, then turn out and cool completely on wire rack.

Top with fresh raspberries.

Chocolate, Chocolate, and More Chocolate Cake

Preheat oven to 350 degrees.
Grease 9x13 inch pan and dust with cocoa.

Cake:
1-3/4 cups flour
2 cups sugar
3/4 cup cocoa powder
1-1/2 tsp. baking soda
1-1/2 tsp. baking powder
1/4 tsp. salt
2 eggs
1 cup boiling water
1 cup milk
1/2 cup vegetable oil
1 tsp. vanilla

Combine dry ingredients (flour, sugar, cocoa, baking soda, baking powder, and salt) in mixing bowl. Add eggs, milk, oil, and vanilla and beat for 2 minutes. Add boiling water and mix to combine. Batter will be very thin.

Pour into pan and bake 35 to 40 minutes until toothpick inserted into center comes out clean.

Remove from oven. With a wooden spoon handle or whatever similar implement is available, poke holes all over the top of the cake and set aside.

Filling:

1 can sweetened condensed milk
1 cup semi -sweet chocolate chips

Place chocolate chips in mixing bowl and set aside. Heat sweetened condensed milk in microwave in 30 second intervals until steaming. Pour over chocolate chips. Whisk until smooth.

Pour chocolate mixture over cake and spread to fill holes.

Set aside to cool (about an hour) then refrigerate until completely cooled.

Whipped Cream Topping:

2 cups heavy cream
1/2 cup powdered sugar
1/4 cup cocoa
1 Tbsp. vanilla
1-1/2 cup mini chocolate chips

Beat cream until soft peaks form. Add powdered sugar, cocoa, and vanilla and continue beating until stiff peaks form. Spread onto cooled cake and sprinkle with mini chocolate chips. Store cake in refrigerator. If you decide to substitute M&Ms for the chips because they're so pretty, eat immediately. The coloring looks disgusting when it merges with the chocolate cream. I know whereof I speak.

Chocolate Caramel Peanut Butter Cake

Preheat oven to 325 degrees. Line spring-form pan with parchment.

Cheesecake layer:

15 mini peanut butter cups, chopped into pieces
1/2 cup butter, softened
1/2 cup sugar
2 (8 oz) pkg cream cheese, room temperature
1 (3 oz) pkg cook and serve vanilla pudding mix
2 eggs
1 tsp. baking powder
1 Tbsp. lemon juice

Cream butter and sugar. Add cream cheese and stir until smooth. Combine pudding mix and baking powder then add to cream cheese mixture. Add eggs, one at a time, then lemon juice. Beat until smooth. Fold in peanut butter cups.

Pour batter into pan. Bake one hour. Remove from oven and place in freezer.

Increase oven temperature to 350 degrees.
Grease 9-inch cake pan and dust with cocoa.

Chocolate Cake Layer:

1 cup flour
1 cup sugar
1/2 cup cocoa
1 tsp. baking powder

1/4 tsp. salt
1/2 cup buttermilk
1/4 cup oil
1 egg
1 tsp. vanilla
1/2 cup hot water

Put flour, sugar, cocoa, baking powder, and salt in mixing bowl. Stir until well mixed.

Add buttermilk, oil, eggs, and vanilla and beat on medium speed until mixed.

Add hot water and blend on low speed.

Pour into pan and bake for 35-40 minutes until toothpick comes out clean.

Cool on rack.

Caramel:
Option 1:
Purchase two jars of Chipotle Caramel Sauce from my friend and gourmet cook, Jon Ashmore, at:
https://squareup.com/market/gourmetfocus-dot-com

Option 2:
1 can sweetened condensed milk
1/4 cup butter
40 caramels, unwrapped

Heat all ingredients in microwave at 30 second intervals until smooth.

Take cheesecake layer from freezer and remove from pan. Line pan with plastic wrap then set cheesecake layer back in pan. Pour half caramel mixture over cheesecake layer and return to freezer.

Remove chocolate cake layer from pan. Line pan with plastic wrap then set chocolate layer back in pan. Pour remaining caramel mixture over chocolate layer and place in freezer.

Leave cakes in freezer for at least three hours or even overnight. When caramel is firm, remove chocolate layer and set on plate. Remove cheesecake layer and set on top of chocolate layer. Return cake to freezer.

Frosting:

1-2/3 cup semisweet chips
1-1/2 cups cream
1 heaping tsp. corn syrup

Melt ingredients in microwave at thirty second intervals, stirring after each interval, until chips are almost melted. Continue to stir until mixture is smooth.

Remove cake from freezer and pour thin layer of mixture over top of cake. Return cake to freezer.

Beat remaining chocolate mixture until light and fluffy.

Frost cake with this mixture. Top with miniature Reese Peanut Butter Cups. Store in refrigerator until ready to serve.

About the Author:

I grew up in a small rural town in southeastern Oklahoma where our favorite entertainment on summer evenings was to sit outside under the stars and tell stories. When I went to bed at night, instead of a lullaby, I got a story. That could be due to the fact that everybody in my family has a singing voice like a bullfrog with laryngitis, but they sure could tell stories—ghost stories, funny stories, happy stories, scary stories.

For as long as I can remember I've been a storyteller. Thank goodness for computers so I can write down my stories. It's hard to make listeners sit still for the length of a book! Like my family's tales, my stories are funny, scary, dramatic, romantic, paranormal, magic.

Besides writing, my interests are reading, eating chocolate and riding my Harley.

Contact information is available on my website. I love to talk to readers! And writers. And riders. And computer programmers. Okay, I just plain love to talk!

http://www.sallyberneathy.com

Made in the USA
Columbia, SC
19 February 2019